THE ANCHOR CROSS TWINS

Richard G. Edwards

Cover Photo

The photograph on the front cover, taken by the author, is a view of Harlan, Kentucky as viewed from Ivy Hill.

Acknowledgements

I feel truly blessed to have such a wonderful wife and friends willing and able to take the time and effort to review **The Anchor Cross Twins**. My wife Carolyn, and dear friends Dr. Bill Green, Dr. August Peters, Dr. Carl Peters, and Mr. Jack Sterling were most gracious and efficient in accomplishing this task. The layout of the book is the expert work of Mrs. Kelly Elliott. She and her wonderful family now reside in Naples, Italy, but through the miracle of the internet she continues to apply her expertise. Many, many thanks to all.

Dedication

My wife Carolyn and I have been greatly blessed to have five wonderful grandchildren. Teagan, Jackson, Cooper, Clayton, and Lillie Edwards all live in Eustis, Florida with their parents, Giles and Heidi Edwards. I dedicate this book to them.

Preface

If you have read any of my previous Anchor Cross books, ***The Anchor Cross*** (now also available as ***The Anchor Cross Second Edition***), ***The Pelle Anchor Cross***, or ***The Helena Anchor Cross***, you are aware that the theme of the books revolve about six anchor crosses that were cast by Roman Emperor Constantine the Great in 325 A.D. using gold that was traced back to being blessed by my Lord Jesus Christ and then given to Saint Peter to help start the church.

The Anchor Cross Twins continues with that theme. I would encourage my readers to share their thoughts and comments with me. My email address is:

richardglennedwards@gmail.com

If you would like copies of my previous Anchor Cross books, please either contact me at the above email address, or you may order them from:

www.BookLocker.com   *The Anchor Cross*

www.Amazon.com   *The Anchor Cross*
                        The Anchor Cross Second Edition
                                The Pelle Anchor Cross
                              The Helena Anchor Cross

www.BarnesandNoble.com   *The Anchor Cross*
                        The Anchor Cross Second Edition
                                The Pelle Anchor Cross
                              The Helena Anchor Cross

May God Bless, and Pax Tecum!

Richard G. "Dick" Edwards
Lexington, Kentucky, 2015

Chapter 1

Paris, France

Air France flight 1800 had just lifted-off from Paris' Charles de Gaulle airport for the two hour flight to Madrid, Spain. Renee Dubois sat in a window seat toward the rear of the plane. She felt lucky to have even been able to get a ticket on the 3:25 pm flight. She also felt lucky that there was no one in the two seats next to her. She wanted to have the two hours to gather her thoughts for the upcoming interview she would have this evening. It would likely be the most important one of her career. As she watched the beautiful French countryside passing below, her mind reflected on the events of the day.

Renee was a feature writer for the Paris based newspaper **Le Monde**. She was 38 years old, attractive, and single. Her career demanded all her attention. After college she spent about 4 years working for a smaller newspaper in central

France and then applied to **Le Monde**. Surprisingly, she was hired. She had now been a feature writer for the Paris newspaper for 13 years. As she sat at her desk just before noon this morning she received a phone call that prompted her to catch this flight to Madrid. She was so excited she could hardly wait. When she landed at the Madrid Barajas airport she would be met by a chauffeur to drive her to the estate of two sisters in the lineage of the French Royal Family. She would have dinner with the sisters, and then listen to their story about two very unusual artifacts. After the interview, she would spend the night in the mansion and then be driven back to the airport tomorrow morning to catch a 7:10 am flight back to Paris. Hopefully, she would be carrying a story that would spread like wildfire across the globe. Renee Dubois could feel a giant leap in her career just around the corner! A Nobel Prize vision was dancing in her head!

She knew that her articles about the beautiful golden anchor crosses were the reason the sisters had selected her for this interview. She had covered in great detail the appearance of three of these anchor crosses in the U.S. The first, called the Seibert Anchor Cross, had been discovered in a remote mountainous area of Harlan County, Kentucky about 13 years ago. The second, termed the Pelle Anchor Cross, was discovered in a church in Prato, Italy and brought to Lexington, Kentucky just a little over a year ago. And then the third, the Helena Anchor Cross, was found in a chapel on the island of Mahe in the Seychelles archipelago in the Indian Ocean only a few months ago, and was also brought to Lexington, Kentucky. Dr. Randy Peters is Director of the

University of Kentucky's Center for Appalachian Research (CAR). He became involved with research on all three anchor crosses, and currently had all three on display in the CAR. It was through Dr. Peters' research that the origin of the crosses had been uncovered. In 325 A.D. Constantine the Great was Emperor of Rome. Largely influenced by his Christian mother, Helena, Constantine converted to Christianity and in 313 A.D. his Edict of Milan decriminalized Christian worship throughout the Roman Empire. In 325 A.D. Constantine had a vision that lead him to produce a symbol that would become associated with Christianity. He combined the anchor, a symbol for religion from well before the time of Christ up to the time of Constantine, with the cross. Before Constantine crosses were not a religious symbol since only the worst of criminals were crucified on them. Constantine changed that. From his vision he had his craftsmen produce a mold that combined the shapes of an anchor and a cross, combining religious symbols from the past and present. In this mold gold would be poured to produce beautiful anchor crosses. These were about 4 inches wide, 6 inches long, and one half inch thick with a hole toward the top of the vertical cross member through which a necklace could be inserted. And each had an inscription on the horizontal arm of the cross that read **Pax Tecum**, Latin for "Peace be with You". Dr. Peters determined that Constantine had produced six of these. which Constantine called the Savior's Crosses. He had made the crosses from one bar of gold given to him by Pope Sylvester I. The bar of gold was very special. It was one of many that had been given to St. Peter after having been blessed by our

Lord Jesus Christ to help start the church. These golden bars were called St. Peter's gold. After producing the six Savior's Crosses Constantine kept one and gave the other five to Pope Sylvester I. Dr. Randy Peters had identified the three, now resident in his Center for Appalachian Research, as being from among those five given to Pope Sylvester I. Renee now had reason to believe the sisters she was on her way to interview had possession of the other two.

If the sisters did in fact have possession of the last two Savior's Crosses given to Pope Sylvester I, her story about them would be given top billing by media all around the world. These artifacts were very, very special. Stories surrounded each of the previously discovered three crosses as having a strange and mysterious power, which had been demonstrated on many occasions by preventing harm to those possessing them. Indeed, if one was wearing a Savior's Cross the inscribed words **Pax Tecum** seemed to be assured for the wearer. In every instance where this power had been demonstrated the anchor cross became heated, apparently somehow associated with energy being liberated through the artifact.

Renee continued to think about how she would handle the story. If the sisters' artifacts appeared to be the real thing, and if the story behind them could be documented, then she would still have to be very careful before releasing a story that would claim these two artifacts to be the last of those given by Constantine to Pope Sylvester I. There was only one person in the world that could determine beyond any doubt if the sisters' crosses came from Constantine. That person was Dr. Randy Peters. Without his authentication there would always be doubt that the anchor crosses were the real thing. Renee thought about this, and then decided that if everything else looked good, then she would contact Dr. Peters to see if he would be willing to come to Madrid to inspect the sisters' anchor crosses. That would involve several more days before she could release the story, but she decided that it would be time well spent. Nothing could be worse for her than to release a story that might prove to be false. If that happened, she could kiss her career good-bye. There were certainly a lot of very good forgeries floating around, and she just had to make certain that the story she would write would prove to be totally accurate. She just hoped that the sisters' story panned out, and, if so, that she could entice Dr. Peters to make the trip to Madrid.

She spent the remaining time on the plane making a list of questions to ask during the interview. She just felt certain that this was her big chance to grab that once-in-a-lifetime story. She wanted to do everything possible to assure all went well.

The two hours passed quickly. The plane began its descent into Madrid.

Chapter 2

Madrid, Spain

As Renee descended on the escalator to the baggage claim area she immediately spotted the chauffeur. He was dressed in uniform as one would expect, and was holding a sign that read "Renee Dubois". Since she only had her carry-on and laptop computer she bypassed the baggage carrousel and walked immediately to the driver.

"Hi there, I'm Renee," she said.

He responded, "Good evening Mademoiselle Dubois. My name is Julien. I hope you had a pleasant flight."

"I did," replied Renee. "It was short and sweet. I'm so anxious to meet the Carmen sisters."

"Mademoiselle Elisabeth and Mademoiselle Henriette are very excited about meeting you. Please allow me to carry your bag and we shall be on our way," Julien replied.

"You may take my carry-on. I'll tote my laptop, thanks," Renee said, and the two of them departed the terminal.

Renee's eyes got very large when she saw the most impressive limousine that Julien was driving. It was a very large, black Mercedes with a sliding glass panel between driver and passenger compartments.

Julien opened the door for Renee and she seated herself in the limo. He then placed her carry-on in the front passenger seat and seated himself behind the wheel. They began their journey.

The sliding glass window between driver and passenger compartments was open and Renee asked, "How far is the estate?"

"About a 30 minute drive," Julien replied. "And it's along a very pretty route. I think you'll enjoy the scenery."

Renee sat back and did just that.

In a short time the limo turned off the road onto a more narrow one that was marked with a sign that said "Private Drive". They drove another mile or so on this road and came to a large gate with a gatehouse adjacent. The security person in the gatehouse immediately pressed the button to open the gate when he saw Julien driving up.

Julien waved and shouted, "Thanks Harry!"

Harry smiled and waved through the gatehouse window.

After rounding a couple of curves lined with thick shrubs the road made a beeline for the mansion about a quarter of a mile off. And a mansion it certainly was!

"Wow," said Renee. "What digs!"

"I too never fail to be impressed by the sight of the

mansion, Mademoiselle Dubois, and I see it from this perspective several times each day," Julien offered. "It has about 50,000 square feet of living space, 15 bedrooms with private baths, and most all the little extras you would expect in a dwelling this size. I think you'll be comfortable here!"

"I could easily do a story on it alone," Renee responded. "This is a bit more than expected."

Julien drove up the circular drive-way and parked by the front entrance. He jumped from the limo and walked around to open the door for Renee. After grabbing her carry-on the two of them walked to the entrance door and rang the doorbell. In short order a maid answered the door with a giant smile and said, "Welcome to The House of Carmen! My name is Marie. Of course I know Julien and assume you must be Mademoiselle Dubois. Mademoiselle Elisabeth and Mademoiselle Henriette are anxiously awaiting you in the parlor. If you will please follow me."

"Thank you so very much," replied Renee. When she saw that Julien was not following them she said, "Julien, thank you so much for the delightful ride. I'll look forward to taking it in the other direction in the morning. See you then!"

Julien smiled and said, "The pleasure was mine. Your carry-on will be in your bedroom. I'll be ready when you are tomorrow morning."

•••

Marie opened the door to the parlor and walked in with Renee in tow. The sisters were seated, but stood when the door opened.

"Ladies, may I present Mademoiselle Renee Dubois," Marie said, then she nodded to the sister on the left and said, "This is Mademoiselle Elisabeth Carmen." Then she nodded to the right and said, "And Mademoiselle Henriette Carmen." Each sister extended their hand to Renee, and then Elisabeth said, "Thank you Marie, we're just so excited to have Mademoiselle Dubois visit us. Please, let us be seated."

Marie then said, "I will bring tea." And she excused herself.

As Renee was taking her seat she carefully observed the sisters. In the few minutes she had before leaving Paris she had tried to research them, but was unable to find much information. She did know that the sisters were twins, had never married, and were 75 years old. They were descendents of the French Royal Family and had lived together outside Madrid in The House of Carmen for their entire lives. Their parents, the Duke and Duchess, had passed on several years ago.

Renee said, "Ladies, please call me Renee."

Elisabeth replied, "And we insist on your calling us Elisabeth and Henriette. Even though your plane trip was only a couple of hours, we know you must be tired. So why don't we just have a cup of tea and do the chit-chat for a few minutes and then allow you an hour to rest before dinner and our meeting afterwards, if that would be suitable."

"Yes," replied Renee. "That sounds good. Please do allow me to say how impressed I am with your beautiful estate. It has far exceeded my expectation! I told Julien that I could do a story just on it. It is certainly lovely beyond description."

"Thank you, my dear," said Henriette. "We do very much enjoy it."

Marie returned with tea service. After tea and a few minutes of small talk Renee was shown to her palatial bedroom where she rested until dinner was served at 8 pm.

•••

Just a couple of minutes prior to 8 pm Marie knocked gently on Renee's bedroom door. Renee was anxiously awaiting the knock, and immediately opened the door ready for dinner. She followed Marie to the beautiful dining room.

The sisters were standing on the opposite side of the table from Renee. The table seemed small in the huge dining room, and obviously had been arranged just for this meal. Renee could imagine the usual size table in the room. Probably large enough to seat 30 to 40 people. But tonight it was just the cozy three of them, and the small table was most appropriate.

The sisters were in identical dresses and shoes. They still looked exactly alike, except for hair styles. Elisabeth wore her hair in a traditional style while Henriette wore hers pulled back into a bun. They were tall, perhaps about 5'9" and thin. Each had gray hair. They had piercing blue eyes. Their voices sounded almost the same. They had an air about them that was befitting their station in life.

Elisabeth said, "Please lets be seated. I hope your brief rest was beneficial Renee."

"Sure was," Renee replied. "But to tell you the truth, I was so excited that I could only lie on the bed and close my eyes and think about all that has happened to me today and all that is yet to come. This has been the most excitement I've experienced in one day in my entire life."

Elisabeth responded, "Henriette and I are equally excited. We think the story we have to tell you this evening will be one that will be worthy of your time and effort. But first, let us give thanks to the Lord for all our many blessings, including this upcoming meal. Then, after we eat, we will retire to the parlor to have our meeting."

"Sounds great," Renee said. It was apparent to her that Elisabeth did most of the talking for the twins. Henriette just smiled and nodded as Elisabeth talked.

After their prayer, lead by Elisabeth, a meal was then served that Renee would long remember. She lost count as to the number of courses, but enjoyed each greatly.

• • •

The sisters and Renee had finally settled in the parlor for their meeting. All sat in plush, comfortable chairs. Elisabeth and Henriette sat side-by-side facing Renee. There was a table between them.

Elisabeth started the conversation, "Renee, I'll begin by giving you a little history that Henriette and I think is pertinent to our story. I don't mean to bore you with family history, but I think after hearing it you will understand its significance."

Renee replied, "Believe me, you'll not bore me! I hope you don't mind my recording our conversation." She had placed a small voice recorder on the table between them.

"No, no, not at all," replied Elisabeth. And she began the story.

"Our great, great, great, and I lose track of how many 'greats', grandfather was King Louis XV of France. He reigned from 1715 to 1774. In 1727 his wife, Marie Leszczynska, gave birth to twin girls at the Palace of Versailles. The girls were named Elisabeth and Henriette. The twins were raised in Versailles, but unfortunately each died at an early age due to smallpox. Henriette passed at age 24 on February 10, 1752. Elisabeth succumbed on December 6, 1759 at the age of 32. Their father, King Louis XV, was devastated by losing the twins. Around the time of Elisabeth's passing there was a great deal of turmoil in France about the presence of the Society of Jesus, or Jesuits. There was a move afoot to have the Parlement de Paris expel the Jesuits from France. In 1761 the King supported the Society. Pope Clement XIII was very motivated to do all he could to support the Jesuits in France, and he decided to make a substantial gift to King Louis XV expressing his thanks to the King for his support. But the Pope did not want the gift to appear as a bribe, so after a meeting at the Vatican between the Pope and Christophe de Beaumont, Archbishop of Paris, the decision was made to offer a gift to the King in memory of his departed twin girls. The Pope gave the Archbishop two beautiful golden anchor crosses to present to the King, one in memory of Elisabeth and one in memory of Henriette. In December, 1761 there was a congregation of bishops assembled at Paris. The Pope thought that this would be a good time to present the gifts, and apparently it was. Just after receiving the golden anchor crosses from the Archbishop the King promulgated a royal order permitting the Jesuits to remain in France. Unfortunately for the Jesuits, the tide of public opinion later turned, and in 1764 the King finally was forced to expel the Society from France. The King was greatly moved by the gift of the two anchor crosses, and he treasured them throughout the rest of his life. Ironically, King Louis XV died in 1774 from smallpox. The two golden anchor crosses, and the story behind them, continued to pass from one King to the next. Our parents, the Duke and Duchess of Carmen, finally became the recipients of these gifts. 75 years ago our mother gave birth to twins, and Henriette and I were named after the twins of King Louis XV. Our parents decided that upon our 25th birthday they would present us with the golden anchor crosses, and tell us the story behind them, and they did. And now I've shared that story with you, Renee. Henriette and I read with great interest your excellent stories in **Le Monde** describing all the activities in the U.S. with the other three anchor crosses, and we decided that the time had come to share our story. We want you to write it for us."

"I'm just almost speechless," replied Renee. "I feel so honored that you would want to allow me to present your story. I hope you won't mind my asking, but would it be possible to see your anchor crosses?"

Responding in unison, the sisters each reached toward the table before them. They each carefully opened a drawer and withdrew a stunning golden anchor cross with a beautiful gold and jeweled necklace. They then held their anchor crosses to Renee.

The color seemed to drain from Renee's face, and her mouth fell open. Her eyes became large as saucers. She tried to speak but the words seemed stuck in her throat. Finally, after inspecting both of the beautiful artifacts, she was able to say, "Ladies, words cannot describe their beauty. I have seen photographs of the three currently held by Dr. Randy Peters, but the pictures simply do not come close to conveying their magnificence. I'm simply in awe! Never in my life have I beheld anything this stunning."

Henriette smiled, nodded, and then said, "We agree!"

Elisabeth then said, "I know you have heard the stories about the mysterious occurrences that were attributed to the other three anchor crosses. Henriette and I can attest to the fact that they do indeed seem to have very special and unexplainable powers. We have experienced such on several occasions, and would like to share with you one each. Henriette, why don't you go first."

Henriette looked a bit shy, but started to tell her experience.

"Although Elisabeth and I are descendents from the French Royal Family, when we were younger we were like most normal girls. We enjoyed doing all the regular things that girls do. When I was about 35 years old some of our friends asked if I would help them in a charity fund raising event. The event was conducted in a large convention center in Madrid, and I believe about 10,000 tickets were sold. Various celebrities appeared, including several rock bands that were popular at the time. My part on the program was simply to introduce one of the celebrities. Being much younger and somewhat foolish, I decided that I would wear my necklace with the golden anchor cross attached. When I made my appearance the oohs and aahs were heard throughout the center for my beautiful golden anchor cross. When the event was over and as I walked to my car in the center's parking structure I was confronted by a robber. It was dark, and the lighting wasn't very good in the garage, but I saw him coming at me out of the corner of my eye. He was wearing a set of those things I believe are called 'brass knuckles', and his right fist was coming really fast toward my face. Just at the moment before impact with my face a very, very strange thing happened.....something I've relived and remembered daily. His fist seemed to strike an invisible stone wall. I heard the bones in his wrist break, and I even saw a piece of his broken wrist bone protruding from the skin. He screamed in agony and fell to the floor. Blood was everywhere. Two things I recall after that. One, I remember that the anchor cross on the necklace around my neck felt very warm to my chest, and two, I started running back inside the center to get help from security. Everything turned out fine, but I know without a doubt that my wearing that anchor cross protected me from the robber. For sure, there is power in the cross!

Your turn Elisabeth."

Elisabeth then started her story, "We had been given our anchor crosses and the story behind them by our parents when we turned 25 years old. It was just a couple of years after that when I was driving my car with several friends. We had been to a party, and being even more foolish than Henriette I decided to wear my anchor cross to impress my friends. I must say, though, they certainly were impressed! But after the party we were driving home and I was traveling down a major highway at about the speed limit when I was distracted for a moment and took my eyes off the road to look at something the girl in the passenger seat wanted to show me. When I returned my eyes to the road it appeared to be too late. An oncoming truck in the opposite lane was, for whatever reason, coming directly at me. I froze, and just knew we would all be killed by the impact with the large truck. It was at that moment that control of the steering wheel seemed to be taken from me and the wheel made a sharp turn. We just avoided the collision. We learned later that the truck driver had fallen asleep. Although both vehicles did wreck, no one was seriously hurt. And like with Henriette I vividly recall that my chest felt very warm where the anchor cross rested. Without a doubt, this was another instance where lives were saved somehow related to the power associated with the cross. That power took control of my steering wheel and turned it to avoid certain disaster. I still don't understand it, but I do know it happened and I will never forget it."

"Wow," Renee said. "Those stories are fascinating."

"They are," replied Elisabeth. "We tell them to you so it will help you understand how our anchor crosses relate to those reported in America."

Renee then said, "Well, I can tell you that I certainly now believe that these anchor crosses were indeed made by Constantine the Great. I feel certain they are the real thing. But during my flight here today I carefully considered that when we arrived at the point where we currently are it would be necessary to try and get Dr. Randy Peters to agree to come to Madrid to inspect your anchor crosses. Without his authentication, when the story goes public there would likely be skeptics that would not think your anchor crosses are real. Would you agree to allow me to contact him to see if he would be willing to come here to inspect your anchor crosses?"

To that Henriette responded, "Oh my, I think that would be very exciting. Do you really think he might come?"

"I just don't know for sure," replied Renee. "I have never talked with him, although through the stories about the other three crosses I feel almost like I know him. My guess would be that with his great interest in the anchor crosses he would definitely jump at the chance to examine yours."

Renee then continued, "One thing that might sweeten the kitty, so to speak, would be if we could show him a photograph. Would you have a problem if I took a picture of the two of you holding your anchor crosses?"

"That's a very good idea," said Elisabeth. "That would definitely get his attention, but I think you need to be in the picture also. I can get Marie to take it."

"I'm game," Renee said as Elisabeth called for Marie.

Renee stood in the center, with Elisabeth on her right and Henriette on her left. They stood with their backs to an ornately decorated wall and Marie took several pictures using Renee's camera. In each the sisters had their anchor crosses hung about their necks and they held the artifacts out lying in the palms of their right hands. Renee thought that these pictures would certainly grab Dr. Peters' attention and could later be used in her story.

Elisabeth then looked at her watch and said, "Ladies, it's getting late and Renee has to get up early tomorrow morning for her return trip to Paris. As much fun and as exciting as it has been, perhaps we should consider retiring for the evening."

Renee said, "Exciting is hardly adequate to describe it for me. I know I'll have trouble sleeping tonight thinking about everything that's happened today. Just imagine, this morning I had absolutely no idea that any of this was about to occur. I just can't thank you ladies enough. But I do have one last question for you. Exactly why did you decide to make your story public? After all, compensation is not an incentive for you, and when the story goes public you will undoubtedly incur a lot of intrusions. So why did you decide to do it?"

This time Henriette spoke up, "Renee, Elisabeth and I are strong Christians. We believe in spreading the word about our Lord Jesus Christ. We think that the power that resides in these golden anchor crosses somehow is related to His blessing bestowed on the gold from which they were made. Certainly we don't understand exactly how this works, or even why it works. But we have experienced it firsthand and we know it exists. We talked about contacting you after reading your reports about the American anchor crosses, and discussed the ramifications of going public. We just decided that these beautiful golden anchor crosses represented lights that we had to let shine. We want the world to know they exist. We thought that somehow by doing that we would be furthering His mission, and that perhaps someone hearing our story would come to accept Him. Maybe I haven't explained this adequately. Elisabeth, do you have anything to add?"

"No sister, I think you spoke well," said Elisabeth.

Renee replied, "I think so also. I now feel I understand why you called me, and why you elected to have your story told. Thank you so much. As soon as I get back to Paris tomorrow I'll be in touch with Dr. Peters, and I'll keep in contact with you regarding anything I find out. Until we get his blessing, the story will stay under wraps. Please do feel free to call me if you have questions. I know you have my number."

"Thank you Renee, we truly appreciate your working with us on this," said Elisabeth. "Let's now retire for the evening, and Marie will knock on your door tomorrow at about 5 am.. We'll have a quick breakfast and then Julien will drive you to the airport to catch that 7:10 flight to Paris. Sweet dreams!"

•••

It seemed almost like she had just rested her head on the pillow when there was a rap on her door and Marie said, "5 am, breakfast awaits."

After breakfast Julien had already gathered Renee's carry-on bag from her bedroom and was waiting to drive her back to the airport. After a good round of hugs and good-byes, Renee departed The House of Carmen. The trip went quickly, likely due in large part to the early hour, and she had no problem at all in making the flight.

As Renee looked out the plane's window at the Madrid landscape passing below she thought, 'What a miraculous 24 hours!'. She could not wait to get to her office in Paris and start to put this story together. The first thing she would do would be to send an email to Dr. Randy Peters inviting him to Madrid to inspect the anchor crosses. The email would have a brief description to go with the attached picture of her with the Carmen Sisters holding the anchor crosses.

Chapter 3

Frankfort, Kentucky

The four were seated at a round table in a conference room at 700 Capital Avenue Bay #100. It was the governor's office in the Kentucky State Capitol Building. Present for the meeting were Governor Brad Shear, Economic Development Secretary Helen O'Malley, Fred Knapp, Mayor of Harlan, Kentucky, and Dr. Randy Peters, Director of the University of Kentucky's Center for Appalachian Research in Lexington.

Governor Shear opened, "I want to sincerely thank Mayor Knapp and Dr. Peters for taking the time to meet today with Secretary O'Malley and me. I believe our meeting will prove very important to the people of Eastern Kentucky. Let me say at the outset that I plead guilty to being a politician, and a part of what we will hopefully accomplish today is motivated by my political side. That being said, let me also say that I would not be supporting today's proposed action unless I thought it would be extremely beneficial to the Commonwealth, and more particularly to the people of Harlan County and Eastern Kentucky. Secretary O'Malley, would you like to set the stage for our proposal?"

"Thank you Governor," Helen O'Malley replied. "I feel like I'm preaching to the choir on this, but please bear with me. Since the two of you were closely involved with the two Anchor Cross events previously held in Harlan I'll not need to go into a lot of detail about these. As you know, both events occurred in October. The first was the Pelle Anchor Cross ceremony that was held on October 10th two years ago this coming October. Although that event did draw a very large crowd, it was somewhat overshadowed by the large explosion that occurred near the end of the ceremony. The second event was last October 5. The Helena Anchor Cross was featured then, and a huge crowd turned out to view it in the Seibert Anchor Cross Memorial on the grounds of the Harlan County Court House. With the single exception of the vulgar display that was carried out by a drunk in line to enter the Memorial, that event went extremely well. What the Governor and I are going to propose today follows along similar lines to the previous two events. Please allow me to just go ahead and say what we have in mind, and then we can discuss it. We would like to propose an annual event in Harlan that would be called The Anchor Cross Festival, or 'ACFes' for short. Governor, perhaps you would like to pick up here."

"Thank you Helen," responded Governor Shear. "We

would propose that the ACFes be an annual week-end festival held on the first week-end of October each year. Although lots of additional events could be scheduled starting on Friday and ending on Sunday, the big show would be on Saturday and would feature a viewing of all the anchor crosses in the Seibert Memorial. A ceremony would be held on a stage constructed on the Harlan County Court House steps and would feature various noted speakers and entertainers. Those attending could view the beautiful golden anchor crosses by filing through the Memorial, which, as you are aware, is located in the Northwestern corner of the Court House property. Now let me quickly add that I feel sure that you're concerned about security for the event. After all, each of those anchor crosses contains over $100,000 worth of gold alone, not to mention their tremendous historical value. But let me assure you that I will make certain that they will be totally safe. If Dr. Peters is agreeable, I will have them transported to Harlan in an armored car with two Kentucky State Police cars escorting ahead and behind it. And I will assign six state troopers to guard at the Memorial. In addition, I'm sure that Sheriff Sterling will provide assistance from his office, as will the Harlan City Police and other state troopers from Post 10 in Harlan. We'll have enough security there to protect Fort Knox."

As the Governor spoke, Dr. Randy Peters' mind wandered. He thought about the history of those two previous events. It was well over 13 years ago that the first of the golden anchor crosses was discovered. Deputy Sheriff Kyle Potter, then a 10 year old boy, found it while hiking in a remote area not too far from the present town of Wallins in Harlan County. Through his research, Dr. Peters had determined that the artifact had been brought into the county by Rev. Karl Seibert in 1798. Rev. Seibert and his wife Mary were killed by an Indian raiding party, and the anchor cross was found by Kyle Potter as he searched through the decayed remains of the Seibert's covered wagon. Then, through a strange turn of events, the Seibert Anchor Cross was instrumental in uncovering 3.5 million dollars of illegal drug money in a botched Harlan bank robbery, and the county distributed these funds to Kyle Potter for discovering it, to Dr. Randy Peters to house it and continue research at the Center for Appalachian Research, and to Harlan County to construct the Seibert Anchor Cross Memorial building on the grounds of the Harlan County Court House. Then, just about 18 months ago, a second anchor cross was discovered in Prato, Italy. It was owned by Domenico Pelle, a wealthy descendent of the famous Pelle vineyards and winery just outside Prato. Mr. Pelle accompanied Randy and the Pelle Anchor Cross to Lexington to verify that it was indeed one of the Savior's Crosses. It was after all the publicity associated with this anchor cross that the Governor and Economic Development Secretary organized a ceremony in Harlan that would draw a large crowd and help with the town's economy. Through another very strange turn of events a suicide bomber attempted to kill hundreds at the ceremony, but failed when assistance came from the mysterious power of the Pelle Anchor Cross and from one of Harlan County's most notorious crooks who learned of the plot and decided he didn't want to see hundreds of innocent people murdered. And finally, only about 6 months ago a third Savior's Cross, the Helena Anchor Cross, was featured in a ceremony at the Seibert Memorial. This third anchor cross had been found in The Seychelles. Randy and its owner, Felix Faure, traveled with the artifact bringing it back to the Center for Appalachian Research for authentication and further research. The Helena Anchor Cross was then featured at another ceremony in Harlan just last October 5. At that ceremony Bennie, the town drunk, was used in a scheme to try and kill Harlan County Sheriff J. Bert Sterling. Bennie was a decoy. To draw attention away from the Sheriff who was in the Memorial, he dropped his pants and 'mooned' people in line at the Memorial to view the anchor cross. During this disturbance Eagle Eye Looney, a hired assassin, had arranged for his friend Badass Brown to attempt to spray the Sheriff with acid, but the plot backfired when once again the mysterious power of the Helena Anchor Cross intervened to save the sheriff. Indeed, the previous events in Harlan associated with the anchor crosses were quite memorable. Randy's mind was then brought back to the present by the words of the Governor.

"............ so I'm here to announce today that the Commonwealth of Kentucky is prepared to support and spend whatever reasonable funds are required in order to make the ACFes a reality. I know there are a lot of questions, and there will be many details that will have to be addressed. I would suggest that Mayor Knapp take the lead in this effort, and he might wish to appoint a committee that would have the responsibility to oversee the ACFes. I'd be interested to hear your reactions."

Mayor Fred Knapp replied, "Governor, Madame Secretary, I know you are aware of my devotion to Harlan. I think the ACFes idea is wonderful. I would predict that thousands would come to attend. Your idea of having a variety of well known speakers and entertainers would simply 'sweeten the pot', so to speak, to the draw of the three mysterious, beautiful, and historical golden anchor crosses. I would predict a huge economic boom for our county, and the publicity that the event would generate would tend to assure its continued success from one year to the next. I congratulate you on having this idea. I'll be delighted to work very hard to help make it a reality. Your thoughts Randy."

Dr. Randy Peters said, "I echo your remarks, Fred. I am concerned with security, but with the assurances the Governor has given us I feel sure they will be safe. One question, did you think we could get started with the first ACFes this coming October?"

Secretary O'Malley replied, "Yes, we would definitely like to get underway immediately. We have about 6 months to put everything together. If we can do that, then the Governor and I think the economy of Eastern Kentucky will receive a big boost."

Mayor Knapp responded, "We'll make it happen!"

he four continued to discuss plans for the ACFes for about another hour, and then adjourned to go their separate ways. Randy and Fred had driven from Lexington together in Randy's car. Fred had made the 3 hour drive to Lexington from Harlan early in the morning, and left his car at Randy's house after the two had met there. The drive back to Lexington from Frankfort gave them additional time to talk about details of the ACFes. One of the things they talked about was the committee recommended by the Governor. Fred asked Randy if he would agree to serve on the committee. Randy agreed and said he would come to Harlan in a week or so when they had their first meeting. The rest of the trip back to Lexington was consumed with talk about the astounding beauty of the Bluegrass horse farms.

Chapter 4

Lexington, Kentucky

Randy had enjoyed a good night's rest after the meeting in Frankfort. As was his custom, he was up early this morning and had arrived at his office around 7 am. He had just gotten a cup of coffee and sat at his desk to review his email.

He first started not to read it, but for some reason he decided to open the email from a Renee Dubois with the Paris newspaper **Le Monde**. He got floods of emails from newspapers around the world wanting information for stories about the anchor crosses. Most of these he passed on to Joyce, his secretary, to process. But the subject line on this email read *'New Savior's Crosses found'*. That got his attention. And when he opened it he saw a photograph that caused him to spill his coffee. It was a picture of three ladies, with the ones on each side holding what looked exactly like Savior's Crosses. He ran to get another cup of coffee .... he could hardly wait to read the text.

*Dear Dr. Peters, My name is Renee Dubois. Likely you don't remember me, but I did correspond with you previously regarding stories that I wrote for **Le Monde** about the three Savior's Crosses that you now have in your Center. Yesterday I received a phone call from two sisters that live outside Madrid saying they had in their possession two of the Savior's Crosses and wanted me to fly there to hear and see their story. I did, arriving yesterday afternoon, and flew back to Paris this morning. The sisters are the Carmen twins, descendents of the French Royal Family. Their story was mindboggling. I would hope you would give me a call and I'll relate it to you in detail. The bottom line is that I am convinced they are in possession of two Savior's Crosses. We agreed that I would not release a story until the crosses could be authenticated. I told the sisters that you were the only person qualified to make that judgment. My phone number is on the heading of this email, and I would hope you would call to further discuss all this.*

Randy's hand was shaking with excitement as he called Mademoiselle Dubois. It was now about 7:30 am in Lexington, and 1:30 pm in Paris. Should be a good time to catch her, he thought. She answered.

After introductions, Renee related her story to Randy.

Based on what she just told him and the very clear photograph of the sisters holding the anchor crosses, Randy was convinced that he would make the trip to Madrid. If these crosses did prove to be genuine, that would leave only one of Constantine's six Savior's Crosses unaccounted for. This was a trip he had to make.

"Mademoiselle Dubois, that is indeed an incredible story," Randy said. "Your story and the photograph certainly have convinced me that I need to come to Madrid to meet with you and the sisters and to examine the artifacts. But I must caution you that if after my close inspection they appear to be genuine, I would need to take them to my Center for final definitive determination. That can only occur by making several tests that establish that they were indeed cast in the molds of Constantine. Do you feel the sisters would allow that?"

Renee replied, "I really don't know. It was their idea in the first place to make their story public, so I would think they would welcome whatever was required to assure that it was true beyond any doubt. Frankly, I think they would have to make that determination after meeting you and accepting your assurances for the safety of the crosses."

Randy said, "That makes sense to me. I can certainly understand why they would be extremely careful. Based on all that I now know, I would like to book a flight that would get me to Madrid tomorrow to meet with you and the sisters, and then return on Thursday. Do you think that would work?"

"Oh my, that is speedy!" said Renee. "I can make it work for me, but I'll have to contact the sisters to see if that would suit them. Can I call you back just as soon as I can contact them?"

"Certainly," Randy replied. "And I must tell you that I'm extremely excited about all this. It certainly is mindboggling that 5 of the 6 Savior's Crosses may now have been located. I can hardly wait to meet you and the sisters. I'll be anxiously awaiting your phone call. Many thanks for all your help, and it was a delight to meet you via the telephone!"

Just as he hung up the phone Joyce arrived for work and stuck her head in his office to say "hi". She saw the astonished look on his face and asked, "Randy, are you okay?"

"I think so," he replied. "Just had a most interesting phone call. Would you kindly check to see how soon you can get me on a flight to Madrid?"

•••

About an hour later Joyce pressed the intercom and said to Randy, "You have a call on line 1 from Renee Dubois."

"I'll take it, Joyce, thanks," replied Randy.

"Yes Mademoiselle Dubois, that certainly didn't take long!"

"Please call me Renee, Dr. Peters. And yes, I was fortunate to be able to talk immediately with Elisabeth Carmen, and she said she and her sister would be most pleased to have the two of us as house guests, arriving tomorrow and departing on Thursday. If that suits you, please have your secretary contact me with your flight number and I'll pass that along to the Carmens. They will have their chauffeur, his name is Julien, meet you upon arrival and drive you to their estate. They will do the same for me. Is that okay with you?"

"Perfect. And Renee, please call me Randy. From what you told me about the House of Carmen, fitting us in probably was not too much of a problem! I'll look forward greatly to seeing the estate as well as the Savior's Crosses and to meeting the twin sisters. Joyce, my secretary, is working as we speak to make flight reservations for me. She'll email you the flight and arrival time shortly. I'm looking forward to meeting you as well, and I sure thank you for all your help with everything. I feel certain you'll be rewarded by getting an exclusive story that will draw great international attention."

Renee said, "Randy I'm just so excited I'm sure I'll have trouble sleeping tonight! My previous stories and research on the Savior's Crosses have me pretty much up to speed on them, and to be involved in locating two more and to have the chance to also meet the world's leading authority on them certainly has my juices flowing."

"Thanks for the compliment," Randy replied. "Since finding that first one I have pretty much devoted my professional career to them. They are fascinating beyond belief. To know that the gold from which they are made was once blessed by my Lord Jesus Christ and then passed through the church, and in 325 A.D. Pope Sylvester I gave one of the golden bars to Constantine the Great to mold into 6 of the anchor crosses certainly has held my interest for well over 13 years now. Thanks again for your help, and hopefully I'll see you tomorrow in Madrid!"

•••

After updating Joyce on everything that had happened, Randy asked her to please try and get Governor Shear on the phone.

"The Governor is on line 1," said Joyce.

"Governor, thanks so much for taking my call. I've got some late breaking news on the anchor crosses that I wanted to share with you."

"Always have time for you Dr. Peters," said Governor Shear. "If you'll permit me I'd like to also get Secretary O'Malley on the phone to listen in. That'll keep me from having to try and remember and repeat what you're getting ready to tell me."

"Great idea, Governor, I'll wait until you get her," Randy replied.

After a brief wait the Secretary got on the line and Randy related to the two of them what had transpired this morning, and that he would be going to Madrid tomorrow to check out the story and the artifacts.

Secretary O'Malley then said, "That is just astounding! This could well develop into yet another great story of international interest from Kentucky, and if these two anchor crosses are the real thing then I could see the possibility of their also being present for the ACFes. I know I'm getting way too far ahead for now, but at least that could happen. And if it did, the publicity surrounding them would draw floods of people to Harlan in October."

"Absolutely correct," said the Governor. "Dr. Peters,

thanks for keeping us posted. You have a great trip tomorrow, and we'll be anxiously awaiting hearing from you when you return."

"Thanks Governor and Madame Secretary, I hope I'll have some good news to share with you when I get back," Randy replied. He hung up the phone, sat back in his chair and thought, 'how very fortunate I've been with getting breaks to uncover these Savior's Crosses. And this trip tomorrow could be a double bonus. I'll likely have trouble sleeping tonight'.

Chapter 5

Harlan, Kentucky

Mayor Fred Knapp sat at his desk in a small office in the back of Creech Cafe. In addition to serving as mayor, Fred owned and operated the restaurant, a hallmark in Harlan. He had inherited it from his father and had started working there after graduating from Harlan High School over 53 years ago. Fred was approaching birthday number 72, and had served as the very popular mayor of Harlan for over 8 years.

His phone rang.

"Fred Knapp speaking, may I help you," he said.

"Hey Fred, Randy here. I take it you made it back to Harlan okay."

Fred spoke, "Dr. Peters, good to hear your voice again. Yes, made the beautiful journey back home without incident, thanks. To what do I owe the pleasure of your call this fine spring afternoon?"

"Well, there has been a development on the Savior's Crosses front, and I thought I'd better give you the update. It could well impact your planning for the ACFes," Randy replied.

Randy then went on to tell Fred all about his conversation this morning with Renee, and then about sharing it with the Governor and Secretary.

"Well, well .... that is a potentially very significant development," Fred replied. "If the anchor crosses are indeed the real deal, then our little festival could be greatly impacted, particularly if it worked out that they could be brought to Harlan along with the other three for display. We might not have enough room for people to even walk on our streets! What a delightful thought! I do certainly thank you for keeping me posted on this. Just like the Governor and Secretary, I'll be looking forward greatly to hearing back from you after your trip ..... I guess that would be most likely on Friday, since you'll probably be getting back to Lexington late on Thursday evening."

"Sounds about right," replied Randy. "I'll call you ASAP, and I'm still planning on coming to Harlan one day next week for our first ACFes committee meeting."

"Good," Fred responded. "You take care on your trip, and I'll hope to hear from you Friday. Thanks again for calling."

After he hung up the phone Fred looked through the glass window in his office out into his cafe. As was usual, there were lots of school kids that had stopped by after school to chat and chew. Creech's was a very popular hang-out, not only with the young set but also with the old timers. Many regulars stopped by daily to have coffee and sit and talk about Harlan, Kentucky, and world problems, and to offer up their solutions. The cafe had a long counter with stools as well as many tables. It had two special features. One was a large green parrot that was now about 24 years old. Fred loved ole Polly, and had built her a rod above the entrance door where she usually perched. Polly had a good vocabulary, and could call several of the regular customers by name. She mooched food anytime a customer would part with a tidbit. At one time there was some question as to whether a parrot could legally be in a restaurant where food was served, but when the question was put on the agenda at a city council meeting it was quickly resolved when about a hundred locals showed up in support of Polly. The second very interesting feature was that Fred had collected interesting stories and photographs over his 53 years at Creech's and had posted them on the walls. All of the walls were literally plastered with these. Some were in frames, some were just cut from newspapers (mainly from the **Harlan Daily Enterprise**), some were pinned up with push-pins, some were fastened with scotch-tape, etc. But once a photograph or story was put on the wall it was there for good. No one could ever remember Fred taking any of them down, and everyone wondered how many more he would be able to put up. The walls were rapidly filling. Fred loved to have customers ask about any of these. He enjoyed greatly telling the story behind each one. And Fred was a very good story teller.

Creech Cafe was located on Central Street in downtown Harlan. It was directly across from the Harlan County Court House. In addition to the usual offices located in a court house, the department of the Harlan County Sheriff, J. Bert Sterling, was located there. The Sheriff and his deputies frequently walked across the street to have coffee with Mayor Knapp in Creech's.

The Harlan County Sheriff's Department was small, and necessarily so. It's budget had been decreasing for years due to the exodus of people due to lack of jobs. Harlan County's principal industry was, and is, coal, and the demand for it had been decreasing as well as the number of persons required to mine it, due largely to automation. Coal jobs reached their peak around 1940, when the population of Harlan County was over 75,000, and the town of Harlan had over 5,000 souls. Since then the census had recorded a steady decline such that by 2010 the county recorded only 29,278 and the town just about 1,600. The tax base was shrinking accordingly. Sheriff J. Bert Sterling's department consisted of only the sheriff and five deputies in Harlan and an additional five deputies in a satellite office in the town of Cumberland, about 25 miles Northeast of Harlan on highway 119. Both offices operated only two shifts, day and evening. Calls to the Sheriff's Department after the evening shift were directed to the Kentucky State Police.

Upon entering the front entrance door to the Sheriff's Department in the Harlan County Court House there was a large reception room. Immediately beside the entrance door was a desk for Deputy Kyle Potter on one side and a desk for

Deputy Simpson Brown on the other. Beyond these there was a long counter, behind which one could usually find Deputy Rosie Cain. Rosie was sometimes called upon to perform law enforcement duties but for the majority of the time she functioned as the Department's receptionist, secretary, and bookkeeper. Deputy Brown normally functioned on patrol and was seldom in the office. Deputy Kyle Potter was Sheriff Sterling's principal side-kick. Kyle had been a deputy for about one year, having graduated from Eastern Kentucky State University's Law Enforcement Program. Kyle was 24 years old. When he was 10 years old he had found the Seibert Anchor Cross while hiking in a remote section of the county near the town of Wallins. Events surrounding that discovery had resulted in his being given a 1.5 million dollar reward, which was placed in a trust fund controlled by his mother, Carolyn, until he reached the age of 21. Some of these monies were used for his college education. Sheriff Sterling was very fond of Kyle, and jumped at the chance to hire him when, after his completing the Law Enforcement Program, Deputy Ape Cornett left the Sheriff's Department to join the Kentucky State Police. Kyle was appointed to replace Deputy Cornett. J. Bert Sterling's office was entered through a door in the back of the reception room. There were two other rooms behind the Sheriff's office. One was for storage, records, and small meetings. The other was a small holding cell.

Sheriff J. Bert Sterling had been a devoted law enforcement officer since graduating from Harlan High School. He was now 62 years old. He had served as a deputy for 15 years, and then decided to throw his hat in the ring to run for Sheriff. He was elected overwhelmingly, and had little trouble being re-elected in subsequent elections. He was very well liked by the people of Harlan County. Bert was tall, thin, and quite handsome. He had never married, and was constantly sought after by the ladies. He took his job very seriously, and was devoted to it. Bert was well aware of the bad image that Harlan County had gotten in past years, and was determined to change that. He was well along the way to accomplishing that goal.

The second shift in the Harlan Sheriff's Department consisted of Deputies Mousy Giles and Bill Black. Bill usually patrolled, and Mousy could usually be found behind the counter in the reception room to answer calls and greet anyone walking into the office, and would sometimes occupy Deputy Kyle Potter's desk.

The final occupant of the Sheriff's Department was very, very special. She had four feet and the best looking fur coat in Harlan. Her name was Preacher Puss. She was a large, gray tabby cat that Rosie had adopted about 15 years ago. Rosie named her Preacher Puss after she was brought to the office by firefighters. She had been found in the smoke filled back room of a church that had caught fire. When found she was screaming at the top of her lungs. The firefighters tried to locate her owner, without success, and brought her to the Sheriff's office. For Rosie it was love at first sight. She immediately convinced Bert that the department needed a mascot, and he agreed to let her stay. Rosie called her Preacher Puss because she was found screaming in a church.

Rosie made an extended trip to Wal-Mart to purchase all the cat necessities, including a nice bed, scratching post, litter box, food, and a good supply of the cat treats called 'Whisker Lickins'. Preacher Puss was immediately adopted and loved by all in the department. Bert built her a shelf located above and to the side of the entrance door and over Deputy Kyle Potter's desk. She loved her shelf, and would bound there by jumping onto Kyle's desk and then on up to the shelf. She would lay there hours on end swishing her tail and watching what was going on in the office, and by looking through the window would keenly observe outside activity as well. All those familiar with her would reach up and give her a gentle stroke anytime they entered or left the office. She would always respond with a loud purr, and swish of her tail.

Soon after adopting Preacher Puss it was discovered that she had one strange, but most appropriate and welcome, peculiarity. She hated guns. This was first discovered when soon after Preacher Puss's arrival the then Deputy Ape Cornett was sitting at his desk (the one currently occupied by Kyle) and decided to clean his gun. When he pulled his gun from his holster with his right hand he suddenly heard a loud scream and then felt sharp pain as the big cat jumped from her shelf onto his right arm with claws extended and dug in. He dropped the gun and Preacher Puss immediately let go his arm and jumped back to her shelf, curled-up, and closed her eyes. And then on several occasions since, she had demonstrated the same behavior when crooks came into the office holding a gun. Sheriff Sterling had declared her to be the lowest paid and most efficient deputy on his payroll.

Her fame had grown among the local law enforcement community, and she was very well known to the people in Harlan.

●●●

Fred looked up from his bookkeeping and saw Sheriff Sterling and Deputy Potter walk into his cafe and take a seat at a table up front. Polly greeted them with a loud, "The law's here, the law's here!"

Bert replied to Polly, "Quiet bird, we don't have food."

Fred came bounding out of his office, grabbed a carafe of coffee, and walked quickly to the table where Bert and Kyle sat.

"Afternoon guys," Fred greeted as he poured coffee into their cups. "Want anything other than coffee?"

"Not for me," Kyle said. Bert shook his head.

Fred took a seat at their table and said, "You two are just who I was getting ready to contact.....can I conduct a little business during your coffee break?"

"Yes sir, Mr. Mayor," replied Bert. "Go right ahead."

Bert started, "As you two know, Randy Peters and I had a meeting with the Governor and Economic Development Secretary in Frankfort yesterday. The reason for the meeting had to do with economic development in Eastern Kentucky in general, and Harlan in particular. They proposed an annual festival held here in Harlan on the court house grounds that they called the Anchor Cross Festival, or 'ACFes' for short. The festival would feature several big name speakers and entertainers, but the highlight would be that all of the anchor crosses now at the Center for Appalachian Research would be brought here for exhibit in the Seibert Anchor Cross Memorial. The Governor promised all kinds of security, and gave us his assurances that nothing would happen to the anchor crosses. He also said his office would cover all reasonable costs associated with ACFes. It sounded like a deal we really just couldn't turn down. So we didn't. Then I get this call just a few minutes ago from Randy saying that he had gotten a lead on two more of the Savior's Crosses, apparently now held by twin sisters in Madrid, Spain. So he's off for Madrid, and if they prove to be the real thing he might have them back in Lexington on Thursday, and it could possibly work out that they could be included in the ACFes. They would certainly generate a lot of world-wide publicity if Randy declares that they are in fact real. It could result in a huge crowd for our first festival, that will be scheduled for the first week-end in October."

"Wow," Bert replied. "You have been a busy little mayor! That all sounds just great if the Governor comes through with enough security to make sure all goes smoothly."

"I think he will," Fred said. "And another thing the Governor suggested was that we form a ACFes committee, one that would have responsibility for overseeing the organization and operation of the festival. He suggested that I chair that committee, and I wanted to ask the two of you if you would please be willing to serve on it. Kyle, you've been associated with this anchor cross thing from the beginning, and are now an integral part of the sheriff's department, and Bert, you've been closely involved in all the anchor cross events here in Harlan. So you two would be naturals. I also am going to ask Raymond Bell, Carolyn Potter, and Jake Keller if they would agree to serve. So that would make it a seven member committee, including me and Randy Peters. What say you?"

"It would be an honor for me," replied Kyle.

"Same here," said Bert. "When do we get underway?"

"Likely one day next week," said Fred. "I wanted to wait to hear from Randy after his trip to Madrid, and then I thought about the middle of next week we could schedule our first meeting."

"Sounds good to me," replied the Sheriff.

"Thanks guys, I knew I could count on you .... but I do sincerely appreciate it," Fred said. "But before you leave, could I tell you the short story that goes with my latest wall posting?"

Kyle looked at Bert, and they both smiled. Kyle then said, "Okay Bert, lay it on us."

Fred got up from the table, walked over to the wall, and pointed to a newspaper article he had just taped up. The headline read 'Man Jumps from Bridge'.

Fred said, "The article is about a man who jumped from the Cumberland River bridge. As he was standing on the rail of the bridge getting ready to jump, a police car happened by and saw him. The officer stopped his car, got out, and said, "Hey fellow, please don't jump. Think of your dear mother and father."

The fellow replied, "They're both dead....I'm going to jump."

The officer then said, "Think of your wife and precious children."

The fellow said, "I'm not married, and I don't have any kids."

"Well, then think about the Harlan Green Dragons and the Kentucky Wildcats," the officer replied.

"Why? I'm from Tennessee and a big Vol supporter," the fellow answered.

The officer replied, "Well, bless your little heart. You go ahead and jump you little rat. You're holding up traffic!"

The three of them roared with laughter. Kyle then asked, "So what happened to the fellow?"

"He jumped," Fred replied. "But the bridge was low and there was a lot of water in the river so he just had a good swim. I think he headed back to Tennessee!"

As Bert and Kyle were walking out the door Polly squawked, "Bye, bye."

Kyle reached up and gave the bird a stroke and said, "Later, Polly."

Chapter 6

Madrid, Spain

Renee was standing with Julien at the foot of the escalator at the Madrid airport. After she had received Randy's flight schedule she was able to catch a flight from Paris that arrived just about one hour prior to Randy's plane. She did that for two reasons. First, she thought it would be silly for Julien to have to make two trips, and second, she wanted to have the time in the limo with Randy to talk further about the sisters' anchor crosses and to get any additional information she might glean from him that could enhance the story she would write for **Le Monde**.

Randy's flight had left Lexington at 6:30 pm yesterday. The 14 hour flight arrived in Madrid at 2:45 pm. Very fortunately for Randy, he was able to sleep on the overnight flight.

Julien was holding a sign that read 'Dr. Randy Peters'. The big grin on the face of the handsome man descending on the escalator looking at Julien's sign told Renee that he had arrived.

He approached the two of them and said to Julien, "You must be Julien, and I would make a wild guess that this pretty lady could be Renee!"

Julien stuck out his hand and said, "You are correct on both counts, Dr. Peters. Please allow me to present Mademoiselle Renee Dubois."

Renee blushed a bit and said, "We've met via the telephone, but it is a great honor to now meet you in person, Randy."

Julien then said, "Mademoiselle Dubois arrived about an hour ago, and I have already loaded her carry-on. Could I take yours now Dr. Peters?"

"Oh, no need Julien, It's small and my only luggage. I can manage."

"Very well, sir," Julien replied. "Shall we proceed to the car?"

The three of them walked outside and to the limousine. Julien then took Randy's carry-on and placed it with Renee's in the passenger seat and they all seated themselves. The sliding glass partition between the front and back of the car was open, and Julien said as they got underway, "As Mademoiselle Dubois is aware, Dr. Peters, we have about a half hour drive to the House of Carmen. I'll close the partition now so you two can talk. If you need to speak to me just rap on the glass."

"Thank you Julien," Randy replied.

The half hour went very quickly. Renee and Randy were

able to learn a little more about each other, and Randy shared with Renee some of the history of his working with the other three anchor crosses.

"Thanks Harry," Julien shouted to the gatekeeper as they entered the drive to the Carmen sisters' estate.

"Oh boy, looks quite palatial," Randy said to Renee.

"Yeah, but only about 50,000 square feet and 15 bedrooms," Renee replied with a grin.

"Sure beats the Best Western," answered Randy.

"And the food and service are 5 star," Renee said.

"I could get accustomed to this," replied Randy.

Julien stopped the limo at the front entrance and opened the door for Renee and Randy.

Marie greeted the two guests and said, "Welcome once again Mademoiselle Dubois, and welcome Dr. Peters to the House of Carmen! If you will please follow me I'll take you to the parlor where the sisters are anxiously awaiting your arrival."

Julien said, "Your luggage will be in your bedrooms. I'll see you tomorrow for the return trip to the airport."

"Thanks, Julien," Renee and Randy said in unison.

Marie led them into the parlor and announced, "Sisters, Mademoiselle Dubois and Dr. Peters."

The twins stood facing the two guests. Elisabeth extended her hand to Dr. Peters and said, "Your reputation precedes you Dr. Peters, it is a genuine pleasure to meet you. I'm Elisabeth, and this is my twin sister Henriette. And Renee, it is so good to see you again. Welcome to the House of Carmen."

After handshakes and hugs all four were seated.

"If it suits you, we thought we would just spend a little time getting to know each other a bit, and Marie will serve tea, and then we'll let you go to your bedrooms to rest before dinner. That would be served at 8 pm. After dinner we can have our discussion about the anchor crosses. Does that sound okay?" said Elisabeth.

"Oh yes," said Randy. "That would be fine, and I must say I'll be very anxiously awaiting both dinner and especially the discussion afterward."

Renee and Henriette nodded in agreement.

•••

After a dinner truly fit for a king, Renee and Randy were taken by the sisters to the parlor to discuss the anchor crosses.

After all were comfortably seated about a round table, Henriette started the discussion by saying, "Elisabeth and I had a talk after our meeting this afternoon, and we both agreed that we feel very comfortable working with the two of you. We feel we can trust you, and that you will always keep our best interest in mind. We know that the two anchor crosses we possess are genuine. They have demonstrated their power to us on several occasions in the past. We also know that in order to establish beyond any doubt that they were cast by Constantine it will be necessary for us to part with them in order that they be tested. We understand that Randy can perform tests in his Center to establish from microscopic analysis that the crosses were formed in the same molds as were used for the other three in his possession. I don't think we have to tell you two how much the artifacts mean to us, but we have decided that we will allow Randy to take both crosses back to Lexington. Further, we have decided that he may keep them in his Center for as long as he thinks they are being useful in his research. We know that the Seibert Anchor Cross is still owned by a Mr. Kyle Potter, the Pelle Anchor Cross is still owned by a Mr. Domenico Pelle, and that the Helena Anchor Cross remains the property of a Mr. Felix Faure. Certainly these three gentlemen have placed their trust in you and your Center, so Elisabeth and I have decided that we will as well. Elisabeth, do you wish to comment?"

Elisabeth said, "Thank you sister. Henriette has pretty much summed up our thoughts. But I would like to offer a couple more. Just as soon as Randy's tests have established that our anchor crosses are real, we want to go on record as giving consent to Renee to release the story to **Le Monde**. Renee has been just super in working with us, and we want to be assured that she will have the exclusive first rights to our story. Secondly, as was the case with Mr. Pelle and Mr. Faure, Henriette and I would like to travel to Lexington to be present for a press conference that would follow Renee's release of the story. And we would be honored to have Renee accompany us on the trip, at our expense. We would plan to leave soon after we received the word from Randy that his testing confirmed our anchor crosses to be genuine. But until Renee releases the story we would want assurances that it would remain under wraps. We would not want any hint of our anchor crosses to be leaked to the media. Is that reasonable?"

Renee looked at Randy. Randy replied, "I am astounded! You ladies are extremely well informed on the previous Savior's Crosses, and I am overwhelmed that you would permit me to take yours back to Lexington. Thank you so much for your trust. All that you say is very reasonable. I would do everything in my power to keep all your wishes. I certainly can understand how close you feel to the artifacts, and I would guard them with my life."

Renee then said, "I concur with Randy. The trust you have placed in me and your extremely generous offer to support me in traveling with you to Lexington touches my heart. I can certainly give you my assurance to try and write an accurate and interesting story of which you will be proud."

"We know you will," said Elisabeth. "And Randy, thank you for your assurances. So now I guess the time has come to again show the twin anchor crosses!"

The sisters once again reached simultaneously to the table in front of them. Opening the drawers they each extracted their anchor crosses and placed them on the table side by side. The golden glow from them was almost too brilliant for the eyes.

Randy spoke, "Those are indeed Savior's Crosses! Just seeing them confirms to me that they are real. There is no doubt in my mind that the testing will confirm that."

Randy then picked up Elisabeth's anchor cross and closely examined it. He noticed that the words **'Pax Tecum'** appeared exactly as they did on the other three. Everything seemed exactly the same. Then he turned the artifact over and examined the back side. He noticed at once an "E" engraved on the top of the vertical member of the cross, above the hole for the necklace. This was something new. The other three anchor crosses did not have such a mark. He said, "I see the initial "E" on the back side of your cross Elisabeth. Do you know anything about it?"

"Oh yes," Replied Elisabeth. "I'm told that King Louis XV had each of the crosses engraved for his daughters, so they would always be remembered. The "E" on mine stands for Elisabeth, and the "H" for Henriette on the back of hers."

"I understand," said Randy as he carefully replaced Elisabeth's anchor cross and picked up Henriette's. In the same location as with the "E" on Elisabeth's, he noted the "H" for Henriette.

"Once again, words are totally incapable of describing the beauty of these anchor crosses," Randy said. "I feel your love for them, and I will certainly do all in my power to protect them. But frankly, I think they're quite capable of protecting themselves. They possess a power far greater than anything mortal."

"We understand," said Henriette. "We've experienced it."

● ● ●

Atlanta, Georgia
"Hey Mr. Mayor, how's everything going in Harlan?"

Randy asked, speaking into his cell phone.

"Well, well, I do believe it is the voice of Dr. Peters," Fred replied. "Are you back in Lexington?"

Randy said, "No, but getting a lot closer. I'm in the Atlanta airport changing planes. I had a little time before boarding my Lexington flight so I thought I'd use that time to update you and the Governor on my trip. I've already called Governor Shear, and spoke with him and Secretary O'Malley, so you were next on my list. I left Madrid this morning at 11 am their time, that was 5 am our time. If my Lexington flight is on schedule I should arrive back home just after 6 pm. Do you have time to hear about the trip?"

"Absolutely," replied Fred. "I hope it's good news!"

Randy went on to tell Fred all that had happened, and wound up saying, "So it now appears that the twin anchor crosses are genuine, and I've got them securely packaged in my carry-on right here beside me. After a few tests in my Center we should be able to definitely pronounce them the real deal, but until then we must keep all this under wraps. I promised the sisters. Once the story and public announcement are released, we should then be able to include them in the planning for the ACFes in October, assuming the sisters agree. I think they likely would, since they've already given their approval for me to keep them in Lexington so long as they are being of value to my research."

"Great news," said Fred. "I've tentatively scheduled the first meeting of our ACFes committee for Thursday of next week. As far as you know, would that suit you?"

"I think that would be fine. I'll clear that day on my

schedule, and look forward to seeing you and Harlan then," replied Randy. "They're starting to board. Good talking with you Mr. Mayor.... you take care."

Chapter 7

Lexington, Kentucky

I t was approaching noon on Friday. Randy sat at his desk thinking about all the events of the past few days. It left his mind spinning. It was almost beyond belief that two more of the Savior's Crosses had been found, and that they were currently being analyzed in his laboratory to establish beyond any doubt their authenticity.

After getting back in town from his Madrid trip last evening just after 6 pm, he had gotten a good night's rest and had arrived at his office this morning at his usual time .... around 7 am. He carried with him the two anchor crosses from the Carmen sisters. His laboratory technician, Rod Bird, was given the two artifacts as soon as he had arrived for work, and Randy had instructed him to immediately drop everything else he was doing and run the necessary tests on the two to establish their validity. Rod was up to speed on all the Savior's Crosses and knew immediately the importance of his tasks. The microscopic analysis tests would establish whether these two new artifacts had been cast in the same mold as the other three now in residence at the Center. And by scraping minute amounts of gold from their back sides he could through some comparison tests establish if they were all from the same material. The tests shouldn't take that long.

"Rod is here to see you Randy," Joyce said over the intercom.

Randy jumped at the sound of her voice, and then said, "Please tell him to come in."

"Hi Chief," Rod said as he walked in carrying the box containing the Carmen Anchor Crosses in one hand and a file folder in the other. He placed both on Randy's desk, took a seat, and then said with a big smile, "All the test results are in that file folder, but I can tell you that beyond a doubt those two anchor crosses were cast by Constantine using the same St. Peter's gold as was used for the Seibert, Pelle, and Helena anchor crosses. They're the real deal."

Randy got a huge smile on his face, and then stood and walked around his desk to Rod. He first patted him on his back, and then shook hands with him and said, "That's the news I was hoping to get, Rod. Thanks for expediting the tests for me."

"No problem," Rod said as he stood and turned to leave Randy's office. "Glad they proved to be genuine."

Once Rod had left, Randy again took his seat and continued to think about what was to happen next. Today was Friday. He thought he would first call Renee and then the Carmen sisters to share the news from Rod's tests. Monday would probably be too early to set up the press conference. Hopefully Renee and the sisters would be able to travel over the week-end, and then have a day to recover prior to the Tuesday press conference. Renee would likely want to release her story to be published in **Le Monde** on Monday, and that would help to generate a lot of interest and attendance at the press conference on Tuesday. And then, If all the ladies were in agreement, they could accompany him to Harlan for the ACFes committee meeting on Thursday.

He punched the intercom and said to Joyce, "Please call Renee Dubois."

Chapter 8

Lexington, Kentucky

It had been a tough six months for Eagle Eye Looney. He had left Harlan immediately following his botched attempt to spray acid on Sheriff J. Bert Sterling, that being his third attempt to fulfill the $10,000 contract made with him by Pretty Boy Maggard to eliminate the sheriff. He knew Pretty Boy would send a hit-man looking for him, so he got in his old pick-up truck and starting driving. He reached Lexington and decided that he could hide there. He didn't have much of the $10,000 left, so he rented a room and started looking for some kind of job. He decided to use the alias of S.C. Yenool. Eagle Eye's real name was Sylvester Calvin Looney, so he used his real initials and then Looney spelled backwards for a last name. The only job he could locate after searching for a couple of weeks was a job as janitor at a small strip mall in the Chevy Chase area of Lexington. The room he was renting was located on a street called Transylvania Park, only about a quarter mile from his work in Chevy Chase. Close enough that he could walk, and that was good since his old pick-up was not the most reliable of vehicles.

The small mall where Eagle Eye worked had only four businesses. There was an ice cream shop, a book store, a souvenir shop, and a jewelry store. Eagle Eye started work each day at 7 am and worked only until noon. All four stores didn't open until 10 am, so he was expected to have each one clean and ready for business daily by that time. The other two hours were usually spent doing outside cleaning jobs. It didn't pay much, but at least it kept him busy and provided enough money for his room and meals.

The jewelry store fascinated Eagle Eye. It's name was 'The Diamond Shack'. It specialized in diamonds, and as Eagle Eye did his daily cleaning there he was captivated by the beauty of the sparkling diamonds in the locked display cabinets. He knew those diamonds were worth big bucks.....he started to think how he might acquire them!

Articles regarding a recent jewelry store robbery in downtown Lexington had been in the newspaper for several weeks, and Eagle Eye had been reading them. Robbers had entered the store carrying a sledgehammer and had forced the employees and customers down on the floor while they smashed the display cases and stole hundreds of thousands of dollars worth of very expensive Rolex watches. It took only 4 minutes from the time the thieves entered until they left the store. The articles in the **Lexington Herald-Leader** described the 'smash and grab' theft as having all the signs of the so called 'pink panther' robberies that had occurred mainly in Europe in recent years. No one was ever hurt in these robberies, but millions of dollars of jewelry were taken. These Pink Panthers were called current day 'Robin Hoods', but rather than stealing from the rich and giving to the poor, they stole from the rich and kept it for themselves. Reading about the Pink Panthers gave Eagle Eye an idea how he might be able to acquire the diamonds in The Diamond Shack.

"Hey Yenool, you're daydreaming again. Get moving.... you've got to have this place all spic and span before we open in about a half hour," said the Diamond Shack's owner to Eagle Eye who had been resting for a moment leaning on his broom as he gazed at the diamonds in the display cases thinking about how they could provide him a nice retirement.

"No problem Mr. Pyle," replied Eagle Eye. "I'll have it so clean you could eat off the floor by the time you open."

"I'll count on it," answered Pyle.

Later that day as he was walking home after work Eagle Eye thought about his plan to rob the Diamond Shack. He knew that the one big advantage he had was to have the keys to the store, and that when he arrived each morning around 7 am there was normally no one there. His plan was to use the 'smash and grab' technique of the Pink Panthers. He would dress so that the security cameras would not identify him, and then use a sledgehammer to smash the display cases having the most expensive diamonds, grab and place them in a bag, and then calmly walk out of the store and to his truck. He knew alarms would go off when he smashed the cases, but he figured he could gather the diamonds and be out of the store in a matter of just a few minutes, and hoped he would be lucky enough that the police would not be able to arrive until later. Once he got to his truck he would head toward Harlan where he planned to take the diamonds to Trigger Green to get him to 'fence' them for him. Trigger operated Maggard's Grocery just outside Wallins, Kentucky in Harlan County. The grocery's original owner, Pretty Boy Maggard, was the very person that had hired Eagle Eye to kill Sheriff Sterling for revenge. Pretty Boy had been forced out of the country 13 years ago after the sheriff had uncovered 3.5 million dollars in drug money that Pretty Boy had stashed in safe deposit boxes in a Harlan Bank. He now lived in Columbia, South America where he continued to operate various illegal operations. Eagle Eye arrived at his rooming house. He thought he'd get a shower, something to eat, and then think more about his retirement plan.

•••

The next day, Wednesday, Eagle Eye had just finished washing The Diamond Shack's windows when he came inside the store to put away his window washing tools and supplies. As he stood in the storage room he left the door open and overheard the owner, Mr. Pyle, discussing an upcoming shipment of diamonds with one of the store clerks.

"They should arrive tomorrow. It'll be the largest shipment we've ever received, with a retail value of around one million dollars. I don't want to have that kind of money just sitting in our display cases gathering dust. We need to sell, sell, sell. I have ads coming out day after tomorrow and continuing for three days in the **Lexington Herald-Leader**. Be sure as soon as the diamonds arrive to make room for them in our display cases and to be ready for showing and selling day after tomorrow," Mr. Pyle told the clerk.

"Yes Sir, will do," the clerk replied.

A large smile formed on Eagle Eye's face. 7 am Wednesday his retirement plan would come together!

Chapter 9

Harlan, Kentucky

The phone rang. Deputy Rosie Cain answered, "Sheriff's office, may I help you?"

Deputy Kyle Potter was sitting at his desk completing some paperwork, but could not help but hear Rosie on the phone.

Rosie then said, "I'll send a deputy right over, thank you, good-bye."

Kyle then said, "Would that mean I'm getting ready to take a little trip?"

"Ole Bennie's at it again," Rosie said. "That was Mrs. Cavanaugh on her cell phone. She said Bennie's drunk and squirting people with a water pistol in front of the post office. Would you mind walking over there and restore peace?"

"I'm here to serve and protect," replied Kyle as he rose from his desk and put on his hat. He reached up and gave a nice, long stroke to Preacher Puss. She thanked Kyle with a loud 'Meow' and a swishing tail, and then closed her eyes to return to her catnap after deciding she wasn't going to get any *Whisker Lickins*.

"Get Bennie's cell ready, I'll have him back here shortly," Kyle said to Rosie as he went out the door to make the short one block walk to the post office.

•••

As Kyle approached the post office on 1st Street he saw ole Bennie, the town drunk, squirt a gentlemen in his crotch as he exited the post office. The gentleman was wearing light brown pants and it now looked exactly like he had just peed on himself. The gentleman looked down at the large, wet spot and started to run at Bennie to grab the water pistol. Mrs. Cavanaugh was standing between the gentleman and Bennie, and as he ran he accidently hit Mrs. Cavanaugh, causing her to drop a package she had just picked up at the post office. When she then bent over to retrieve her package Bennie squirted her directly in the center of her hind quarters. She was wearing a pair of red slacks, and they now had a large, round wet spot on her derrière. Bennie took off running, with both Mrs. Cavanaugh and the gentleman closely behind. When Bennie turned his head to look where he was going he ran into Deputy Kyle Potter.

"Whoa there," Kyle said as he grabbed Bennie.

"Just water," Bennie shouted. "Didn't hurt a thing."

Mrs. Cavanaugh said, "That Bennie is a disgrace to our fair city. You should lock him up and throw away the key!"

The gentleman then said, "I don't live here in Harlan. I was just mailing a letter, but that damn drunk squirted me with his water pistol and then squirted this nice lady. You need to arrest him officer."

Kyle replied, "Now, now.....you all calm down. Bennie did do a bad thing, and I saw him do it as I was walking here. But it is just water and it'll dry quickly. I'll take him to the jail and let him sober-up. I apologize for him. You folks have a good day."

Kyle started to walk Bennie back to the Sheriff's Department as the two victims walked to their cars in a huff.

• • •

Deputy Rosie Cain was seated behind the reception counter getting ready to order some supplies for the Department when the door opened and in walked Bennie with Deputy Potter trailing behind. As they walked through the door Bennie made a big mistake. He pointed his water pistol at Rosie and squirted her.

Bennie then heard the same shrieking sound that he had heard several months ago when he pulled a gun from Deputy Potter's desk drawer when the deputy had left him momentarily. And then the same pain as before stuck again from the top of his head, and gray fur settled over his face. Blood started to flow down his head, and was smeared by a swishing tail.

Preacher Puss dug his claws deep into Bennie's head and continued to shriek. Letting out a loud scream Bennie finally dropped his water pistol. Preacher Puss then jumped from Bennie's head back onto her shelf, laid down, curled her tail around herself, and closed her eyes.

Rosie grabbed the first aid kit and rushed to Bennie to take care of his wounds. Kyle sat Bennie down in his desk chair and tried to calm him. Preacher Puss's attack had quite a sobering effect on Bennie. As soon as Rosie had finished applying the first aid Kyle took Bennie back to his holding cell where he could sleep off both the alcohol and the trauma of Preacher Puss's attack.

Sheriff Sterling walked into the office just as Kyle was returning from placing Bennie in his cell. Rosie and Kyle explained to Bert what had just happened, and they all three had a good laugh.

"Ole Bennie was certainly drunk, but his aim was still right on. He shot both Mrs. Cavanaugh and the stranger in very embarrassing spots, and then shot Rosie right in the face. But Preacher Puss certainly made him pay for shooting Rosie," Kyle said with a grin.

"Yeah. Preacher Puss maintains her stellar record here in the Sheriff's Department. Anyone drawing a weapon around her pays the price," Bert replied.

Rosie added, "It was funny. I know Bennie has injuries, but I bet all that alcohol he consumed helped to lessen the pain. At least there were no serious consequences. All's well that ends well."

Rosie then reached up to Preacher Puss with a handful of *Whisker Lickins*. The cat responded immediately by jumping up and woofing them down with an appreciatively swishing tail. Rosie then gave her several nice pets. She meowed loudly while looking at Rosie with big, alert eyes. She then curled up and continued her cat nap. Just another day's work for Preacher Puss.

Chapter 10

Lexington, Kentucky

The trio saw him as they descended on the escalator going to ground level to retrieve their luggage. Randy had arrived at Blue Grass Field only about 10 minutes ago, and stood at the bottom of the escalator holding a large hand lettered sign that said *'Welcome to Kentucky'.* He hugged Renee, Elisabeth, and Henriette and then said, "What a delight to have the three of you here. I know you must be tired, so after we gather the luggage I'll take you to my home and get you all settled in there. We'll have something to drink and chat briefly and then let you get some rest, if that suits you."

Henriette spoke, "That sounds great, Randy. I worry that we're imposing on you. We could certainly stay in a hotel."

"I would be insulted," Randy replied. "My home is far, far from the House of Carmen, but it is a four bedroom so each of you will have your own private quarters. And frankly, it will work out very conveniently for me, not having to take you to and from the hotel. If not palatial, at least I hope you will find it comfortable."

Renee spoke, "I'm sure it will work great. Do we have kitchen privileges?"

"Fridge is full," said Randy. "And the pantry is too....I don't think we'll starve!"

"Looking down at all the beautiful Kentucky horse farms as we were landing was really quite a sight. I'm looking forward greatly to seeing some of your famous horse country," Elisabeth said.

Randy beamed and said, "We Kentuckians are very proud of the Bluegrass, and I look forward to showing it off to you. Kentucky is indeed a state of geographic diversity. We have many rivers in our state with the famous Ohio River forming its northern boundary. Down in Western Kentucky we have relatively flat land referred to as 'The Purchase'. Central Kentucky is largely the famous Bluegrass, and in Eastern Kentucky we have the beautiful Appalachian mountains. I hope to show these to you in a trip to Harlan after our press conference here in Lexington. But we'll talk about that later."

"What is 'The Purchase'?" asked Henriette

Randy replied, "Technically its called the Jackson Purchase, but most refer to it simply as 'The Purchase'. It's a region in extreme Western Kentucky bounded on the West by the Mississippi River, on the North by the Ohio River, and on the East by the Tennessee River. It gets its name from the fact that Andrew Jackson purchased it in 1818 from the Chickasaw Indians. Technically it was a part of Kentucky at its statehood in 1792, but it was not under definitive control until Jackson made the purchase in 1818."

"I see my luggage," shouted Renee.

"Me too," said Henriette

"And mine as well," said Elisabeth.

Randy retrieved all their luggage onto a cart, and they headed to the parking garage to load in Randy's car.

As they left the airport property Randy said, "Ladies, the land in front of you is called Keeneland. It is Lexington's famous race course. Since we're here, I thought we might just drive through it to give you a little feel for its beauty. Bordering Keeneland on its East side is Calumet Farm, famous for many race horses, including many Kentucky Derby winners. As you landed you likely saw Calumet from your plane. It stands out, being bordered by white fences."

"What Kentucky Derby winners did Calumet have, and where did its name come from?" asked Elisabeth.

As he drove through the beautiful grounds of Keeneland Randy said, "I think they have eight Kentucky Derby winners, including Whirlaway in 1941 and Citation in 1948. These two are United States Triple Crown of Thoroughbred Racing champions. In all, they have 11 horses that have been inducted into the National Museum of Racing and Hall of Fame. Calumet is 762 acres, and was established in 1924 by William Wright, founding owner of the Calumet Baking Powder Company, from which it got its name."

"I can tell already that we are going to learn a lot from

you about Kentucky during our brief stay," Renee said. "And I'm really looking forward to it!"

•••

After they arrived at Randy's home and got all settled they gathered in his living room to have tea and soft drinks and talk a bit.

"Ladies, if you will permit me I'd like to talk a bit about your schedule. After we finish our discussion I'll let you retire to your bedrooms to rest a few hours and then we'll go to dinner around 8 pm. In the morning, Tuesday, we'll go in to my office and we have the press conference scheduled for 10am. We can then spend the rest of tomorrow in my Center, looking at the other Anchor Crosses and discussing the plans for yours. On Wednesday morning I'd like to drive you around the Bluegrass, and then on Wednesday afternoon to Harlan. We'll spend the night with Pastor and Betty Bell. They have a lovely home and plenty of room for us. You'll find them to be extremely hospitable and most interesting. As you're likely aware, Raymond Bell discovered the Helena Anchor Cross about 6 months ago in the Seychelles. Then on Thursday morning I'd like you to meet with a group of friends in Harlan. Technically it will be a committee meeting to get underway with a week-end festival in Harlan that will be held the first weekend in October each year. The governor of Kentucky came up with the idea for the festival, called the Anchor Cross Festival, or 'ACFes' for short. He asked Harlan's mayor, Mr. Fred Knapp, to head-up the committee, and Fred asked if I would serve on it. It will be an excellent time for you to meet several of my good Harlan friends, all of whom are very familiar with the various Anchor Crosses. We would then return to Lexington on Thursday afternoon and let you ladies get a good night's rest before flying out of Lexington back home on Friday. I hope these plans sound reasonable to you."

"Good. Real good," said Elisabeth, as Renee and Henriette nodded vigorously in agreement. "That should accomplish everything we hoped for in the brief time we have. And just in case you were wondering, I would want the three of us to also return to Kentucky in October to participate in the first ACFes, if I'm not being to presumptuous."

"No, no, not at all," said Randy. "As a matter of fact, I think the three of you at ACFes would add greatly to its attraction. I just feel sure that the committee will express this very thought at our meeting on Thursday. So, let's finish our drinks and then let you get a little rest before dinner."

The four continued to talk for another half hour, and then the ladies napped before dinner.

Chapter 11

Harlan, Kentucky

It was Tuesday morning. Fred, Bert, and Kyle sat at their usual table toward the back of Creech Cafe having coffee.

Fred spoke, "I'm sure looking forward to seeing the noon news today on tv. I'm anxious to see the Carmen sisters and to hear their story. Randy called me last night and told me that they volunteered to come back to Kentucky in October to participate with us in the inaugural Anchor Cross Festival. And I assume that means they would also allow their anchor crosses to be on display at the ACFes. Randy also said they would be accompany him tomorrow to Harlan and would be at our ACFes committee meeting on Thursday."

"Good news," replied Bert. "That will give us a chance to meet and get to know them a bit. I hear that even though they are French Royalty, and filthy rich, they are good, decent people. I look forward to meeting them. And like Mr. Mayor said, after their news conference this morning the media will be all abuzz with their stories. I too will be tuned in for the noon news to hear about it. "

"Yes indeed," said Mayor Knapp. "All that publicity will generate lots of renewed interest in the stories of the anchor crosses, and will help greatly in attracting a giant crowd for our first ACFes festival in October."

Kyle said, "It sure will. And I'm looking forward to meeting that French reporter, Renee Dubois. I understand she'll be with the sisters when they come with Randy to Harlan tomorrow."

Fred responded, "Yep, she'll be along too. So, before you guys get back to catching crooks, I did have a new story to pass along, if I may?"

Bert and Kyle grinned at each other, and Bert said, "Go right ahead Mr. Mayor, make our day!"

Fred pointed to a photograph pinned on the wall not far from their table. It was a photo of a lady with a wild hairdo. "You see that lady there with the strange hair? There's quite a story behind her. That's Mrs. Blanton. As I understand her story, about a month ago she went to a hair dresser here in Harlan, and while she was getting her hair fixed she told the hair dresser that she was getting ready to take a trip to Rome, and hoped to see the Pope. The hair dresser said 'Rome? Why would anyone want to go there? Its crowded and dirty. You're crazy to go to Rome. So, how are you getting there?' Mrs. Blanton replied, 'We're taking Continental....got a great rate.' The hair dresser said, 'Continental? That's a terrible airline. Their planes are old, their flight attendants are ugly, and they always run late. So where are you staying in Rome?' Mrs. Blanton said, 'At the nice Rome Plaza.' The hair dresser said, 'I know it....don't stay there. It has a good reputation but it's really a dump.' Mrs. Blanton then said, 'And we're going to the Vatican and hope to see the Pope.' To which the hair dresser replied, 'Ha, that's rich, you and a million other people try and see him. He'll look the size of an ant to you. Good luck on this lousy trip.....you're going to need it.' Two weeks later Mrs. Blanton came back to the beauty shop for another hairdo. The hairdresser asked her about her trip to Rome. She replied, 'It was wonderful. Not only were we on time in one of Continental's brand new planes, but it was overbooked and they bumped us up to first class. The food and wine were wonderful, and I had a handsome 28 year-old steward who waited on me hand and foot. And the hotel was great! They had just completed a $5 million remodeling job, and now it's a jewel, the finest hotel in Rome. 'Well,' muttered the hairdresser, 'that's all well and good, but I know you didn't get to see the Pope.' Mrs. Blanton replied, 'Actually, we were quite lucky, because as we toured the Vatican a Swiss Guard tapped me on the shoulder and explained that the Pope likes to meet some of the visitors, and if I'd be so kind as to step into his private room and wait the Pope would personally greet me. Sure enough, five minutes later the Pope walked through the door and shook my hand! I knelt down and he spoke a few words to me.' The hair dresser said, 'Oh really, what did he say?' Mrs. Blanton said, 'He said, where did you get that terrible hairdo?'."

As Bert and Kyle stood up to leave with big grins on their

faces Bert slapped Fred on the back and said, "Another great story Fred. Just don't ever tell anyone who that hair dresser was...you might get sued!"

"Bye boys, bye boys," Polly said as the sheriff and his deputy left the store.

● ● ●

Lexington, Kentucky

The University of Kentucky's Center for Appalachian Research (CAR) was buzzing with activity. The press conference was about to get underway. The conference room in the CAR was large, and had been arranged with a long table with chairs at one end of the room, and the rest of the room with rows of chairs. Plenty of room was left in the back for cameras mounted on tripods. The room was packed. Bright lights were shining toward those that would be seated at the front table. Reporters from newspapers and television stations over Kentucky, from the Cincinnati and Southern Ohio area, and from Nashville and Knoxville, Tennessee were present. At exactly 10 am a door behind the front table opened and in walked Dr. Randy Peters, Mademoiselle Renee Dubois, and the Carmen sisters. There were four microphones placed on the table in front of four chairs. The quartet took their seats.

"Good morning ladies and gentlemen. I think I know most of you, but for those I've not had the pleasure to meet,

I'm Dr. Randy Peters, Director of the University of Kentucky's Center for Appalachian Research. So great to have such a fine turnout for our press conference. That's a tribute to these three ladies, and to the story that they're prepared to share with you this morning. First, please allow me to introduce them. On my right is Mademoiselle Renee Dubois, a feature reporter for the Paris newspaper **Le Monde**. On my left are the Carmen Sisters, descendents of the French Royal Family. On my far left is Mademoiselle Henriette Carmen, and beside me is Mademoiselle Elisabeth Carmen. The sisters currently reside in Madrid, Spain."

The ladies each nodded and smiled as they were introduced. Camera shutter's clicked and television cameras rolled.

Randy continued, "I should first tell you that the Carmen sisters elected to give Mademoiselle Dubois exclusive first rights to their story. Renee had done a wonderful job of covering the stories of the first three Constantine Anchor Crosses, which, by the way, currently reside right here in the Center for Appalachian Research. So the Carmen sisters chose her as the person they would ask to hear and write their story. She has done so. Today's edition of **Le Monde** is just hitting the streets and carries Mademoiselle Dubois' story. She submitted it to her newspaper yesterday for publication today. Each of you were given a copy as you entered. I'm sure you have had time to read it, and I know that you have questions and comments. But before they give their comments and take your questions, I wanted to ask them to show you their prized possessions. Ladies."

In unison Elisabeth and Henriette opened their suit jackets to reveal the stunning anchor crosses they were wearing on necklaces. The bright lights' reflecting off the golden artifacts were almost blinding. The oohs and aahs from the media filled the room. Everyone leaned forward to get a good look. Flashes from still cameras were like a lightning storm. The Carmen sisters beamed with pride.

After giving ample time for pictures Randy then said, "Ladies & gentlemen, I would next like to ask Elisabeth, and then Henriette, to give a statement. After those, we will take your questions."

The sisters then told the media about their anchor crosses. Questions followed for another half hour.

It was approaching 11 am when Randy said, "I want to thank each of you for taking the time to meet with us today. I appreciate your interest, and I certainly appreciate so very much the Carmen sisters and Mademoiselle Dubois for their participation. We'll now stand adjourned so you can get those stories out."

Chapter 12

Prestonsburg, Kentucky

Big Jim Owens and Mad Mike Hatfield sat in the small office in the back of Big Jim's grimy little gas station. It was located just off highway 23 about a mile south of the town of Prestonsburg, Kentucky. They were watching the noon news on a small television set.

As the news began the screen was filled with a picture of Lexington's channel 27 CBS reporter Barbara Clark. Barbara, a native of Harlan, was describing the morning news conference, "French royalty are visiting in the Bluegrass, and they brought with them two more of the astounding golden anchor crosses."

She went on to relate the stories of the Carmen Twins, and showed lots of video footage taken at the press conference. The camera had gotten excellent shots of the two anchor crosses worn by the Carmens.

"I'll be damned," said Big Jim. "There's two more of those things. Look just like the one we tried to get last October."

Big Jim and Mad Mike had developed a plan last October to intercept Dr. Randy Peters and Helena Anchor Cross owner Felix Faure as they brought the anchor cross to Harlan. Posing as police officers, they stopped Randy's car and attempted to steal the artifact, but were unsuccessful when the amazing and unexplainable power of the anchor cross deflected bullets to render the assailants wounded and helpless. They were fortunate to be able to escape.

"Yeah, two more of those damned things," said Mad Mike. "They look harmless enough, but that one last October sure caused us trouble."

Big Jim Owens was a drug dealer, and into any other illegal activity that would turn a buck. The gas station was just a front from which he operated. Almost 14 years ago he lost $200,000 when his driver wrecked his car while attempting to deliver drug money to Pretty Boy Maggard in Harlan. Pretty Boy laundered drug money for several dealers. Sheriff J. Bert Sterling discovered and confiscated the money when he and his deputies were investigating the wreck. Then a short time later the sheriff discovered 3.5 million dollars in drug money that Pretty Boy had stashed in lock boxes in a Harlan Bank. That money too was confiscated. Big Jim had a strong dislike for the sheriff of Harlan County.

Mad Mike Hatfield, Big Jim's principle crony, said, "But looking at all that beautiful gold sure does get me excited!"

Big Jim seemed lost in thought as he watched the television report.

Finally, Big Jim responded, "Well, well. Two more of those things. I think that makes a total of five that that feller Peters has there at U.K. We screwed up royally last October in trying to get one, but I'm thinking now that we might be able to get all five."

"What you be thinkin Big Jim?" asked Mad Mike.

Big Jim replied, "Don't have all the details in mind just yet, but we still have the snitch that works as a janitor in Peters' Center there at U.K. His name is P Rat Cook. He's the one that passed us information last October about when Peters would be driving to Harlan, and the description of his car. I'm thinking we just might be able to use him to help us pull off a little operation to get those five golden thingys. They'd be worth a mint."

Mad Mike said, "I hope you do remember that when we tried to steal that one last October I wound up getting shot in the ass and you took a bullet in your leg! That golden thingy had some kind of strange power. I don't think we want that kind of trouble again."

"Oh, I remember all that," said Big Jim as he rubbed his leg. "My leg still aches from that bullet. But if we try again we'll have a way to grab them thingys without need for bullets. Give me a little time to develop it.....this time it'll work."

"You smart, Big Jim," said Mad Mike.

"Yeah, I know it," said Big Jim with a smile on his face.

Chapter 13

Harlan, Kentucky

Bert and Kyle were just entering the Sheriff's Department after having Wednesday morning coffee with Fred at Creech Cafe. Rosie had just changed Preacher Puss's litter box, and was replenishing her food and water bowls. Preacher Puss was rubbing Rosie's ankles and purring with satisfaction. Rosie stroked the cat several times and said, "Preacher Puss, you're a lot of trouble, but I guess I shouldn't complain since you're so good at stopping crooks that don't know any better than to pull a gun in here. And besides, you're just a nice kitty."

Kyle took a seat at his desk and Bert said to Rosie, "You be careful what you say to that cat. I wouldn't want her to get the idea she could ask for a raise. You know what a limited budget the office is operating on." Bert joked, and then said, "Kyle, what's on your docket for this morning?"

Kyle was looking at an envelope on his desk, and said, "Well, looks like I got a warrant to serve in Wallins. I've been meaning to drop by to say hi to my grandmother, so since she lives only a short distance from where I'm to serve this warrant I may take the opportunity to stop in for a short visit with her. Mawie's always asking mother about me, and I feel badly that I don't get to see her as much as I would like."

Bert replied, "Yeah, you need to do that. Mawie's one of my favorite people. She must be where you and your mom got all your good genes."

"I guess you're right Bert," Kyle said.

"And while I'm thinking about it, I may just ride with you to Maggard's grocery and stop off for a visit with Trigger Green while you're delivering the warrant and visiting Mawie. I've been meaning to pay him a visit for some time, and this would be as good a time as any. And we can save the taxpayers some money by using only one car. Would that suit you?"

Kyle said, "Hey, I'd enjoy having company. Maggard's is just a mile from Wallins, so it's right on the way. If you don't mind my asking, why do you want to visit with Trigger Green?"

"Well," said Bert, "as everyone in Harlan County is aware, ole Trigger is into a lot of illegal activity. But we've never been able to close him down. He's good at what he does, and he's actually been very beneficial to us recently on at least two different occasions. During the Pelle Anchor Cross program at the Court House he was responsible for switching out the explosives of the suicide bomber and saved many lives by doing so, and then later he gave ole Eagle Eye Looney a faulty rifle that likely saved my life when Eagle Eye tried to assassinate me with it. So I think even though Trigger is a crook, he does have a good heart. So I wanted to drop by just to give him a 'heads up' on the upcoming ACFes next October, and hopefully get him to agree to let me know if he learns of any bad guys planning anything to disrupt it. He does, after all, know about most everything going on in the county, both legal and illegal. And although his operation is not on the up and up, I still enjoy visiting with him and Fatso."

Trigger Green and Fatso Chapel were the only two 'employees' at Maggard's Grocery. The store was just a front for Trigger's various illegal operations. He was into stolen merchandise, drugs, moonshine, credit card theft, and just about anything else that could turn a buck. He had an office in the back of the store. In the front was a modestly stocked grocery, and Fatso Chapel usually sat behind it's checkout counter either reading magazines or watching a small television set. In addition to stocking and operating the store, Fatso had the responsibility to screen people that came into the grocery. Many were there to see Trigger, and for those he would press a button behind and below the checkout counter to release a lock on the door going into Trigger's office. For those that came to shop he would tally their groceries and take their money. Several closed-circuit cameras were mounted outside the store and monitors were located inside where Fatso and Trigger could see and screen anyone parking and getting ready to enter the store. Both Fatso and Trigger had pistols readily at hand should they be needed. Fatso also loved to tell corny jokes. Elephant jokes were his specialty.

"How soon will you be ready to go," Bert asked.

Kyle responded, "How about 5 minutes?"

"Good, gives me time to get rid of some of Fred's coffee, and I'll be good to go," said Bert.

• • •

Lexington, Kentucky

It was time! The alarm clock went off at 6 am, but Eagle Eye was already awake. He didn't sleep well last night thinking about the robbery this morning. He had packed everything he wanted to take with him last night and put it in his pick-up truck. All he had to do this morning was his usual bathroom routine, dress, and drive to work. He had purchased a large sledgehammer at Lowes, and had sawed off the wooden handle so that it fit nicely in a small canvas bag. He planned to use the sledgehammer to bust open the display cases, and then grab the diamonds and place them in the canvas bag. He'd just leave the sledgehammer. He knew that his fingerprints were on everything in his room and at work, so there was really no reason to be careful about them. He figured the cops, and likely the FBI, would trace the robbery to him pretty quickly, but he was counting on being able to get to Harlan and working a suitable deal with Trigger Green to fence the diamonds and provide him cover long enough to fly out of the country with his 'retirement' money. He couldn't wait.

He drove his old pick-up truck and parked it just about a block away from his work. It was far enough that any surveillance cameras would not pick it up. He then got out with the canvas bag and started walking to his work at the small strip mall. It was now just a couple of minutes before 7 am. The door locks at the strip mall were connected to timers that did not allow them to be opened until 7 am each morning. This prevented them from being opened by unauthorized persons having a key. The owners of the stores in the mall had a code that they could enter in a touch pad beside the doors that overrode the timers in case they wanted into their store during odd hours. Eagle Eye was not privy to that code, so he had to wait until 7 am before unlocking the door. He arrived at the door at 7:01 am, opened it, and entered.

As was the usual case at this hour, there was no one to been seen in the mall. He had everything to himself. Lucky so far. He immediately walked to the Diamond Shack, opened the door to it, and walked inside. It was now time to do the deed, and then get out as fast as he could with the diamonds. He figured he had at least 5 minutes unless he was unlucky enough that cops just happened to be driving in the area. That was just a chance he would have to take.

Eagle Eye was wearing a jersey with a hoodie pulled up over his head and was wearing goggles to protect his eyes when he smashed the display cases. He also wore a pair of heavy gloves to protect his hands. He hoped that the hoodie and goggles would keep people from identifying him when reviewing the video from the surveillance cameras. It might buy him a little additional time if they thought the robber had knocked him out and tied him up somewhere.

There were three large display cases that had been crammed full of the one million dollar diamond shipment that arrived yesterday. Eagle Eye had carefully observed where these were placed, and it was only these that he would steal. He didn't have time to try and get others.

He got the sledgehammer from his canvas bag and smashed the first display case. Glass went everywhere and loud alarms began to ring. He then immediately moved to the second case and smashed it, and then to the third. After opening all three cases he threw away the sledgehammer and grabbed the canvas bag and started to pack it with the diamonds. First from the third case, then the second, and finally from the first case. He had all the diamonds, and it had only taken about 4 minutes. He then zipped the canvas bag and headed out the door. He made it outside without seeing another soul, although the alarm was still very loud. He tried to walk calmly, and headed for his pick-up truck. Several cars passed, but the drivers ignored him. He saw two people across the street looking and pointing toward the mall as the source of the alarm noise, but they too seemed to not notice him. He reached his pick-up truck and jumped inside. He placed the canvas bag on the floor of the passenger side and started his engine. He then drove offf slowly, in a direction away from the Diamond Shack. Less than a minute later he heard several police sirens that were getting much louder, but did not pass him. Their intensity then seemed to level off.

They must have arrived at the Diamond Shack from another direction. Eagle Eye smiled, and continued to drive out of Lexington toward interstate 75 South. Ten minutes later he was on the interstate and settled down for the three hour drive to Harlan. His retirement plans were going smoothly.

He looked over at the canvas bag. He could hardly contain his joy in realizing that it contained about one million dollars worth of diamonds.

He looked at his truck's speedometer. He had to be very careful not to break any traffic laws. He needed to do nothing to draw attention to himself. He maintained his speed on the interstate at exactly 70 mph.

He took the first exit at Corbin, Kentucky, getting off interstate 75 onto U.S. 25E headed toward Pineville, where he would take highway 119 to Maggard's grocery outside Wallins. After exiting the interstate he drove about 5 miles and came to a fast food restaurant. He realized he had not had anything to eat, and decided to stop. Not wanting to leave his precious cargo, he ordered from the drive-thru, and then continued his journey. He was now just a little over an hour from Maggard's. Things were looking good.

• • •

Bert and Kyle left the Sheriff's Department, got in Kyle's cruiser, and started their short journey to Wallins. Bert always enjoyed spending time with Kyle. He had known him all of his life, and thought of him as a son. Kyle's mom, Carolyn, was very special to Bert. They had been close friends for many years. Carolyn worked as a teller at Harlan's Miners Bank. She got the job shortly after graduating from Harlan High School. The bank's president, Calvin Brown, had taken her under his wing, and she had developed into a highly efficient and valued employee. Bert liked Carolyn greatly, and the two of them had developed a special relationship.

After driving for about 20 minutes Kyle said, "Well, we're about to Maggards. You give ole Fatso and Trigger my regards. I'll bet you a steak dinner that Fatso will lay an elephant joke on you before you can get through the store to Trigger's office."

Bert replied, "I won't take that bet. I've never been able to get by him without hearing one."

Kyle turned off highway 119 into the parking lot at Maggard's grocery. "I'm not sure exactly how long it will take me to serve the warrant and to visit Mawie, but I'd guess probably about an hour. If you need me for anything before I get back to pick you up just give me a call. I'll keep my cell handy."

Bert Replied, "I'm sure the time will work out fine. Only problem would be if I got stuck with Fatso and had to listen to a litany of his jokes. If that happens I'll give you a call, otherwise I'll just see you when you get finished."

"See you then," said Kyle.

Bert got out of the car and walked into Maggard's. Kyle drove off headed to Wallins.

"As I live and breathe, I do believe our humble establishment is graced by the presence of the Harlan County

Sheriff," Fatso said as Bert walked in the door.

"Hey Fatso," Bert replied. "I need to talk with Trigger, can you push the button to open his door?"

"Of course I can, Sheriff, Trigger's always happy to talk with you," Fatso said. "But can you tell me what is gray, has four legs, and a trunk?"

"Sounds like an elephant to me," replied Bert.

"Wrong," said Fatso. "A mouse going on vacation is gray, has four legs, and a trunk!"

Bert said, "Push the button Fatso."

"Gladly," Fatso replied with a chuckle.

Bert opened the door and entered into Trigger Green's office.

Trigger was sitting at his desk. He had noticed on his security monitor Bert's arrival, and was anticipating his entrance. He stood and walked around his desk and stuck out his hand to Bert and said, "Welcome, welcome, welcome Mr. Sheriff. It is an honor to have you visit me. I hope this is a social rather than a business call."

Bert shook hands with Trigger and said, "Actually it is a combination of social and business, but I can assure you that the business has nothing to do with your operation, my friend."

The two were seated, and after passing pleasantries for a while Bert finally got down to explaining the upcoming ACFes in October and asked for Trigger's help to tell him any potential problems that he might learn about. The two continued to talk.

•••

Eagle Eye saw the Sheriff's cruiser about a quarter mile ahead of him as it turned off 119 onto the road to Wallins. He thought to himself that his luck was continuing....he didn't think the officer driving the car saw him, and that was fortunate since his ole pick-up truck was quite distinctive. He passed the Wallins road and continued on 119 about another mile to Maggard's grocery.

The events that then took place could probably never again be duplicated. Just as Eagle Eye started to turn into the parking lot at Maggards, Fatso felt the need to go to the bathroom. There was no one else in the store, so he had just closed the restroom door when Eagle Eye walked into the store. In the back room, Trigger and Bert had just ended their meeting and the two were standing and saying their good-byes. The monitor in Trigger's office was best viewed from a seated position, and as he and the sheriff stood and talked they did not see Eagle Eye enter the store. Eagle Eye looked over at the check-out counter where Fatso normally sat and noticed that he wasn't in his usual spot. He looked around the store and didn't see him. So he continued walking through the store and toward Trigger's door, thinking he would just knock on it. Eagle Eye was carrying the canvas bag containing the diamonds.

Eagle Eye was just a few feet from Trigger's door when it opened and out walked the Sheriff of Harlan County. Eagle

Eye froze. Bert froze. The color drained from both their faces. Bert then started reaching for his pistol, and Eagle Eye instinctively swung the canvas bag up over his head and then threw it downward as hard as he could to slam against Bert's hand reaching for his pistol. Bert screamed at the impact. Eagle Eye turned and started to run as fast as he could for his pick-up truck, leaving the canvas bag behind. Bert was doubled over and holding his right hand. A toilet could be heard flushing, and Fatso came running out. Bert, Fatso, and Trigger all ran after Eagle Eye, but by the time they got to the parking lot Eagle Eye had made it to his truck and was burning rubber as he headed back onto 119 in the same direction as he came in. Just after Eagle Eye passed the Wallins cutoff Kyle's police cruiser approached 119 coming from Wallins. Kyle saw the back of an old pick-up headed toward Pineville at a good rate of speed, but he failed to associate the truck with Eagle Eye and was focused on getting back to Maggard's grocery to pick up Bert.

By the time Bert got his cell phone out and called Kyle he saw his deputy coming to pick him up. Rather than ask Kyle to turn and chase Eagle Eye, Bert just called Rosie and told her to broadcast an alert for Eagle Eye, and he described the pick-up truck. The state police were immediately notified, as were the city police at Pineville. That old pick-up would be easy to spot. Bert felt confident that Eagle Eye would be caught in short order. The four walked together back into Maggard's grocery.

Fatso said, "Sheriff, I'll get our first aid kit and see if there's not something in it to ease the pain in your hand."

Bert replied, "Thanks Fatso. It'll be okay. I don't think anything is broken, but it sure feels like a brick hit it. I wonder what's in that canvas bag?"

"Since he was carrying it on his way to see me I bet it's something that may be a little shady," Trigger admitted with a shy grin.

Kyle smiled and spoke, "My thoughts as well. How about we just take a look?"

Kyle reached down and picked up the bag and carried it to the checkout counter. He placed it on the counter as Bert, Trigger, and Fatso all gathered around. He unzipped it and they looked inside. Looks of astonishment appeared on their faces.

"Could that be what it looks like?" asked Fatso.

Trigger reached inside the bag and scooped up a handful of the diamonds. "Ouch, he said," and saw a trickle of blood on his hand holding the diamonds. He placed them on the checkout counter.

Bert closely examined them, and said, "I'm no expert, but those diamonds certainly look like the real thing. But I see some pieces of glass mixed in with them. Trigger, I think you cut your finger on the glass. Now Fatso can fix you up with his first-aid kit."

Kyle said, "Wow. If those are real diamonds, there must be a fortune here. The fact that glass is mixed with them would likely indicate that some kind of glass case was busted to get at the diamonds. We need to check to see if there was a robbery recently that would match up."

Fatso left the group momentarily and returned with a

pair of gloves. "Put these on Kyle to protect your hands, and then you can gather them up and put them back in the bag. I'm sure these are now evidence."

"Thanks, Fatso," replied Kyle as he put on the gloves and then while Bert held the open bag at the side of the counter Kyle slid the diamonds and glass back in the bag and then zipped it up.

Bert then said, "It would certainly appear that Eagle Eye was bringing these diamonds here to work something with you, Trigger, to fence them. It certainly won't be hard to find out where they came from. I'll bet there was a very recent robbery somewhere not too far off. We'll know about it quickly, and then will be able to match the diamonds up and get them returned. In the meantime, we'll hold them for safe keeping at the Sheriff's Department."

Trigger said, "Geez, what a morning. A fortune in diamonds shows up in my establishment and I don't net one cent!"

"But you did your civic duty to help us recover the stolen property and hopefully catch ole Eagle Eye......you'll get a big star for that," said the Sheriff.

"Yeah, I really need a big star," said Trigger.

Fatso looked at Bert and said, "Hey Bert, you know what is brown, has four legs, and a trunk?"

Bert just stared at Fatso.

"A mouse coming back from vacation," replied Fatso with a chuckle.

Bert and Kyle took the canvas bag and left Maggards heading back to the office.

•••

Eagle Eye couldn't believe his bad luck. What were the odds of him running into the Harlan County Sheriff in Maggard's grocery. What in the world was Bert doing there anyway? And then to confront him face to face just feet apart! That just couldn't possibly happen. But it did. And to lose all those diamonds. And now every cop in Southeastern Kentucky was looking for him. He had driven about 10 miles from Maggards when he decided to get off 119. He knew that police would be looking for his pickup truck. He had to dump it and then steal another vehicle. At Pathfork, Kentucky he turned off 119 onto state road 72 and traveled South to route 2005. It connected with highway 987 which went West to route 217. Then he picked up route 988 which went South to Cumberland Gap. He felt certain that the police would not be on these back roads. They'd be looking for him on 119 toward Pineville, and then on 25E towards Middlesboro or Corbin. The back roads had bypassed Pineville and Middlesboro.

Just before he got to Cumberland Gap on highway 988 he found a dirt road that lead to a cliff that overlooked a river. He got what belongings he could carry out of his pick up, and then managed to push the truck off the cliff into the river. He then began walking to Cumberland Gap. He figured he had about 5 miles to walk. When he got there his plan was to go the parking lot at the Cumberland Gap National Park headquarters and look for a car to steal. He would then drive the car to Knoxville and meet up with a couple of Harlan buddies that he had kept in touch with. Then he'd try and figure out what he'd do with the rest of his life.

•••

Bert and Kyle arrived back at the Sheriff's Department and checked in with Rosie.

"Anything new on the search for Eagle Eye?" asked Bert

Rosie replied, "Nothing at all. Highways 119 and 25E are crawling with police looking for him, but so far they've had no luck."

Kyle said, "Well, ole Eagle Eye's not the brightest light, but he likely has enough sense to know that his old pick-up would be easily spotted. My bet would be that he ditched it somewhere, and likely either hitchhiked or stole a vehicle."

"I agree," Bert said. "Rosie, how about putting out a 'Be on the lookout for' Eagle Eye Looney, with a description of him and state he's wanted for burglary. Someone might spot him."

"I'll do that Chief," Rosie replied.

Bert then asked, "Any jewelry store robberies been on the news this morning?"

"A big one," Rosie replied. "Channel 27 covered a one million dollar diamond robbery that took place early this morning at a place called The Diamond Shack in Lexington. They had not arrested anyone, and said the investigation was ongoing. Why do you ask?"

Kyle sat the canvas bag down on Rosie's counter, unzipped and opened it, and said, "Want to see what a million dollars worth of Diamonds look like?"

Rosie looked inside the bag and got a shocked look on her face.

"So that's what ole Eagle Eye was up to?"

"Apparently so," Bert replied. "We need to contact the Lexington Police and let them know we think we have their diamonds, but not the thief."

"I'll do that," said Kyle as he zipped up the canvas bag and took it to the safe in the evidence room for storage.

Chapter 14

Lexington, Kentucky

Randy, Renee, and the Carmen sisters were up early on Wednesday morning. Randy was anxious to tour the ladies around the Bluegrass during the morning, and then they would make the drive to Harlan where they would spend the night with Raymond and Betty Bell and then attend the inaugural ACFes committee meeting on Thursday morning. They had all packed their overnight bags and loaded them in Randy's car early that morning.

One of the things Randy wanted the ladies to experience while in Kentucky was to have breakfast at the Cracker Barrel. He thought that would be a good American treat that they would enjoy. Accordingly, on this Wednesday morning they had left Randy's home and were on Man-O-War Boulevard headed to the Cracker Barrel. It was about 7:15 am and as they chatted an old pick-up truck passed them moving at a good rate of speed.

"Some people sure get in a big hurry," Randy said. "And that ole pick-up don't look like the safest vehicle I ever saw .... I hope it makes it wherever he's headed."

After a great Cracker Barrel breakfast Randy toured the ladies all over Fayette County looking at horse farms. The ladies marveled at all the magnificent horses and manicured farms. They went to the Kentucky Horse Park on Ironworks, spent a couple hours there, and then went to a horse farm near Georgetown named Old Friends farm. It kept retired race horses, including many Kentucky Derby winners. There they were able to feed a carrot to Silver Charm, winner of the 1997 Derby. The ladies truly enjoyed the morning tour, but time soon ran out, and they finally began the trip to Harlan.

The trip from Lexington to Harlan normally took around 3 hours. But Randy wanted to make a couple of stops along the way, including getting off I75 at Berea to drive through the lovely town and make a brief stop at the famous Boone Tavern to let the ladies see some of the crafts produced by Berea College students and a chance to see their lovely campus. The other stop was at Corbin where the foursome had a light lunch at the original Colonel Sanders restaurant. They each had to have a fried chicken breast. The restaurant definitely still had the Colonel's secret recipe! They didn't want to have a big lunch because they knew they would be in for a real treat at the Bell's home for dinner. Betty loved to cook, and Randy had told the ladies what a fine meal was in store for them.

They arrived in Harlan around 5 pm. Raymond and Betty Bell were sitting on the porch of their home as Randy drove into their driveway. After introductions, hugs, and kisses they went into the house and were seated in the living room after placing their overnight bags in their bed rooms.

"I do have some sweet tea for you, if that's okay?' Betty asked.

All quickly nodded in agreement, and Renee said, "Thank you very much. We've really become fond of sweet tea since we've been in Kentucky. Randy introduced us to it."

Raymond then said, "It is indeed a very special treat for us to be able to host you ladies. I hope you don't object, but Betty and I have taken the liberty of inviting the other ACFes committee members to join us for dinner tonight. We thought that would be a good way for everyone to meet prior to our formal meeting tomorrow morning."

Again, all the ladies nodded in agreement, and Elisabeth said, "That will work real well for us. I just hope having so many for dinner is not too much of a burden on Betty."

"Oh no," Betty replied. "I consider it a real treat to be able to cook for everyone. Cooking is my thing. I just hope my Kentucky food will agree with everyone."

Renee then said, "So far, everything we've had to eat in Kentucky has been excellent. And I'm sure your meal tonight will be the highlight. Thank you so much for preparing it."

Raymond said, "Dinner will be served at 7. So we have time now to relax and talk."

•••

Badass Brown was at his trailer reading the **Harlan Daily Enterprise**. Usually he just looked at the comics and sports, but an article on the front page caught his eye. It talked about a meeting tomorrow morning at City Hall that would address a new festival that would be held in Harlan on the first weekend of October each year. The festival would be called the Anchor Cross Festival, or ACFes. The paper said it would have all kinds of entertainment, and would feature showing the golden anchor crosses. Huge crowds were anticipated. The committee meeting tomorrow would include Sheriff J. Bert Sterling. Just the mention of the Sheriff's name started Badass's rear quarters, legs, and feet to ache.

It was just last October that Badass had been hired by Eagle Eye Looney to attempt to assassinate Sheriff Sterling by spraying him with sulfuric acid. Unfortunately for Badass, the contraption he was wearing malfunctioned and resulted in the acid running down his hind quarters to his feet. He spent several weeks in the hospital rehabbing. Since there was no proof that he intended to squirt the acid on Bert, he was released when he got well enough to leave the hospital. He had been fuming about getting even with the Sheriff ever since.

Badass knew that the City Hall meeting room tomorrow would be packed with cops, so he couldn't do anything to really hurt Bert there. But as he thought about it, he suddenly had the idea that he could indeed embarrass everyone and perhaps disrupt the meeting. That would at least give Badass some revenge for the acid thing.

He thought about a plan. He decided what he'd do would be to locate the town drunk, ole Bennie, and give him a bottle of whiskey to perform his specialty at the committee meeting. That caused a big grin to form on Badass's face. It would be really embarrassing. He knew there would be some press there at the meeting, at least a reporter from the **Enterprise**. He could just see the article that would be printed in the paper. He laughed out loud.

●●●

The remaining guests started arriving at the Bell's home around 6:30 pm. Kyle and his mother Carolyn were first to arrive, then Jan and Jake Keller, and finally Bert and Fred. The Keller's had become involved when about 18 months ago Mr. Dom Pelle, the owner of both the Pelle Anchor Cross and the famous Italian Pelle winery and vineyard, visited Harlan and discovered that the Kellers had a Harlan County vineyard with grapes capable of producing a wine comparable to his. Dom Pelle then purchased a large tract of land in Harlan County and hired the Kellers to cultivate grapes there that would later be used to produce quality Pelle wine. It was hoped that when this occurred it might prove to be a real boost to the county's failing economy, and hopefully would encourage others to also become involved in planting vineyards and producing wine.

The Carmen sisters had been delighting the guests with stories about their family and about their anchor crosses. Renee DuBois had been actively taking notes on all the conversation, and after Kyle Potter's arrival had been peppering him with questions about his initial discovery of the Seibert Anchor Cross in Harlan County almost 14 years ago. It was a golden opportunity for her since everyone present had some association with one or more of the 5 anchor crosses. The 7 o'clock hour rapidly approached, and Raymond said, "I believe the time has come for dinner. I would appreciate each of you taking a place around the table in our dining room. We'll have a blessing, and then give Betty the opportunity to prove to us what a fine cook she is!"

•••

Thursday morning arrived. The ACFes committee meeting was scheduled to begin at 10 am in the Harlan City Hall meeting room. Because the meeting involved several city and county officials, it was necessarily open to the public. Word had gotten out about the nature of the committee and the topic of the meeting, so a large crowd was expected.

Badass Brown was up early. It didn't take him long to locate ole Bennie. He was hanging out at the coal monument beside the County Court House. He was sitting on it, and his eyes were just about to close. He was about to doze off. Badass punched him in the stomach and said, "Wake up Bennie, I've got a job for you."

Bennie snapped both eyes open and saw that Badass had a bottle of something in a brown paper bag in his left hand. "What you got in that bag, Badass?"

"It's half of your reward for doing a little easy job for me. You do the job right, and I'll give you the other half," Badass said.

'Show me," Bennie replied.

Badass pulled the fifth of whiskey slowly out of the paper bag.

Bennie's eyes got big as saucers, and he said, "I'm ready! What'd you have in mind?"

Badass explained to Bennie what he wanted him to do.

"Oh, that's easy. I can handle that. Give me that first fifth," Bennie said.

Badass replied as he handed Bennie the bottle, "Here it is. Just make sure you do everything just as I told you. Make sure you remember to yell that word as loud as you can when you do the deed. You do remember the word, don't you?"

"Sure," Bennie replied. "The word is 'Attention'."

"You got it," said Badass. "Attention.....and shout it real loud."

•••

Harlan City Hall was located at the corner of First and Clover Streets. The meeting room was fairly large, but today's meeting was going to pack it. Ten people were seated at the long table at the front of the room. Normally the Harlan City

Council occupied these seats. Folding chairs were placed for the audience, with about 30 chairs on each side of a center aisle. Those attending the meeting entered through a door at the back of the room. The room itself was upstairs, on the second floor. Just outside the back door were the stairs.

Seated at the front table were Mayor Fred Knapp and Sheriff J. Bert Sterling in the center two seats. Renee DuBois, the Carmen sisters, and Randy Peters were seated from left to right on the left of center, and Raymond Bell, Carolyn and Kyle Potter, and Jake Keller from left to right on the right of center.

The room was already hot. The air conditioner was having trouble keeping up with the heat from all the people. Deputy Rosie Cain had asked Sheriff Sterling if she could attend the meeting. She was very interested to listen to the Carmen sisters tell their stories, and also to learn about the new ACFes. Rosie had a sister, Posie, who frequently filled in for Rosie when she needed to be away from the office during business hours. The nicknames Rosie and Posie were given to the sisters by their parents. Posie was about one year older than Rosie. Rosie told the sheriff that she would get Posie to watch the office while she was attending the meeting. Unlike Rosie, Posie didn't care for cats. So Rosie thought it would be a good idea just to bring Preacher Puss with her to the meeting. The cat needed to get out of the office anyway. The fresh air would do her good. Rosie had a leash for Preacher Puss, even though the cat would never allow herself to be walked on it. Rosie carried Preacher Puss to the meeting and grabbed a chair on the left side, back row right next to the aisle and door. If Preacher Puss started to act up she could easily slip out without disturbing anyone. She placed the cat on the floor in the aisle next to her, and kept his leash in her left hand. Preacher Puss seemed to be enjoying being there. She sat with alert ears and eyes, watching all that was going on.

Being the gorgeous creature that she was, Preacher Puss drew the attention of those that could see her. One man across the aisle and one row toward the front particularly admired the cat. At exactly 10 am Mayor Fred Knapp looked at his watch and started to stand to offer a welcome to everyone. At that time things happened so fast that they were best described later by the article in the **Harlan Daily Enterprise**. The reporter had gotten the story from the cat admirer across the aisle from Rosie and Preacher Puss. His account was as follows:

At exactly 10 am I was watching the beautiful cat that Deputy Cain had by her side. The cat sat very alert to all that was going on. Suddenly ole Bennie, the town drunk, appeared at the top of the stairs. Bennie walked into the back of the meeting room, turned around, dropped his pants and underwear, and then bent over to 'moon' everyone. He appeared to then take a deep breath and was getting ready to yell something when the cat noticed his testicles swinging like a pendulum. The cat's eyes got real large and she pointed her head right at the testicles. I saw her claws come out, and then she lunged and made a strong swipe that struck home.

The next sound was Bennie's ear piercing scream as he leaped forward to escape the cat. In doing so he lost his balance and went head over heels down the stairs. There was then another scream as his head bounced off one of the stairs. I think the EMTs hauled him off to the hospital with a fractured skull. I hope he'll be okay.

Amazingly, the crowd missed seeing almost all of Bennie's antics, although they certainly heard him. By the time Bennie screamed the first time he was already moving lightening fast toward the stairs, and then he disappeared as he fell down them. Other than the man that gave the account in the paper and Rosie, hardly anyone else even knew Bennie had tried to make the vulgar interruption. The program continued without incident.

The mayor addressed the crowd, "Ladies and gentlemen, it is so good to see this large turnout. Planning for the new annual Anchor Cross Festival that we're launching this morning is very exciting and will certainly greatly benefit our town. Please excuse those screams you just heard.....they came from ole Bennie. I'm sure he's been hitting the bottle again."

The crowd chuckled.

Fred then introduced the three visitors at the head table, and they each talked briefly about the events that brought them to Kentucky. At the end of their talks, the Carmen sisters reached for their anchor crosses in a brief case lying on the table in front of them. As they held them up for the crowd to see gasps could be heard throughout the room. The **Harlan**

Daily Enterprise reporter snapped several photographs. All strained to get a good look at the beautiful golden artifacts.

Next Fred introduced Dr. Peters, and he described his research and findings investigating the two new anchor crosses.

The mayor then covered his meeting in Frankfort with the governor and economic development secretary that gave birth to the ACFes. The remaining time was spent discussing specifics about all the events that would take place in October, and questions and comments were solicited from the audience. The meeting concluded at 11:45 am.

All those at the front table lingered there, and several persons in the audience came up to shake hands and offer additional comments. Finally just the 10 were left. Fred then said, "Folks, I sincerely thank each of you for your participation this morning. I believe the ACFes announcement was well received, and I think we had a great first committee meeting. Special thanks go to Mademoiselle DuBois and the Carmen sisters for adding greatly to our meeting. I'll get back to you when the next meeting is scheduled."

Randy then spoke, "Thank you Mr. Mayor for doing a fine job. I'll be driving the ladies back to Lexington now, they need to get a little rest before they fly back home tomorrow."

Elisabeth said, "It was our pleasure. We enjoyed tremendously our visit to Harlan, and getting to know so many great new friends. I've talked with both Henriette and Renee, and we've agreed that we want to come back for the festival in October. So, you haven't seen the last of us!"

Handshakes, hugs and kisses were exchanged, and then everyone departed City Hall.

•••

Badass Brown had parked directly across the street from City Hall where he had a good view of its entrance. He had gotten excited when he saw Bennie enter just before 10 am. He hoped the disruption would be great enough that all those attending might come running out shortly. To his dismay, the next thing he saw happening was an ambulance arrive and EMTs enter City Hall with a stretcher. He then saw ole Bennie all laid out on the stretcher as they loaded him in the ambulance and sped off. He had a real bad feeling. "Damn," he shouted as he started his engine and started driving home.

•••

Fred, Bert, Kyle, Carolyn, Rosie, and Preacher Puss all walked back to the Sheriff's Department together. Upon entering, Posie immediately wanted to know how the meeting went. Rosie explained that the meeting itself went great, but that there was a little disturbance when Bennie made an appearance just as it was getting underway. Rosie then gave everyone a detailed 'second by second' description of what Bennie did and how Preacher Puss responded. When she finished her story everyone was laughing so hard that tears were flowing down their faces.

Finally Bert looked up at Preacher Puss, now lying contently on her shelf, gave her several gentle strokes, and said, "Ole girl, you certainly are gifted at finding ways to serve the Sheriff's Department."

Preacher Puss responded with a big swish of her tail and loud purr. She then closed her eyes and began yet another of her catnaps.

Chapter 15

Knoxville, Tennessee

Summer was coming to an end. It was the third week of September. Eagle Eye Looney sat in a room with four of his buddies at a junkyard about 10 miles north of Knoxville on route 441. He had been successful in stealing a car at the Cumberland Gap National Park after his escape from Sheriff Sterling, and had driven to Knoxville and located the junkyard operated by his friend Bad Eye Cawood. Bad Eye had previously operated a junkyard just outside Harlan. That had been about 14 years ago when he and his three employees, Snake Potter, Jones Anderson, and Billie Lingal, had attempted a bank robbery in Harlan that failed due to the presence and unexplainable power of the Seibert Anchor Cross. The four were sentenced to 15 years in jail, but were paroled for good behavior after 12 years. Bad Eye used the funds he had received from selling his junkyard in Harlan to purchase the current one in Knoxville. It was a very dumpy little junkyard, but suited Bad Eye. He only wanted it as a base for various illegal operations, including stripping stolen cars for parts and selling moonshine from Harlan County. Snake Potter, Jones Anderson, and Billie Lingal still worked for him. Snake's ex wife and son were Carolyn and Kyle Potter. Carolyn had filed for divorce shortly after Snake was sentenced to prison, and it was granted immediately. Carolyn had tried for many years to reform him. She tried to get him to quit drinking and be a responsible husband and father, but Snake rejected all her attempts. His involvement in the bank robbery and being sent to prison was the last straw. Carolyn and Kyle had not seen him now for about 14 years.

The room where they were seated was the junkyard office. It was dirty, with windows that looked as though they had never been cleaned. There was a small television on Bad Eye's desk, and several small chairs. A grimy coffee maker was located on a table beside a wall. Bad Eye had gotten his nickname after he lost his right eye to disease as a kid. He wore a patch over his nonfunctioning eye.

It was lunchtime, and the five men sat in the office eating sandwiches and watching the noon news on the television set. Their attention was drawn to the news anchor reporting a story from Harlan:

Harlan, Kentucky Mayor Fred Knapp released a statement today describing the upcoming inaugural Anchor Cross Festival to be held on the first weekend of October, only about 3 weeks from now. Mayor Knapp said that the Carmen Sisters from Madrid, Spain would be featured in the festival, called the ACFes. As I'm sure all you listeners recall, the Carmen Twins, descendents from the French Royal Family, are the owners of two of the famous Anchor Crosses, which will be on display at ACFes, and the Twins will participate in a parade and ceremony in downtown Harlan on Saturday, October 6th. Mayor Knapp announced that the other three anchor crosses that currently reside at the University of Kentucky's Center for Appalachian Research will also be on display during ACFes. In addition, the Mayor said that many popular music groups, entertainers, and politicians would be appearing, and that he anticipated a record number of visitors in town for the festival. Additional details are available on our website.

"Hot dang," said Bad Eye. "Sounds like big doings coming up in Harlan."

Eagle Eye replied, "Yeah, everyone really gets all excited over them golden cross things. I wouldn't be surprised if the town was packed."

"You got that look in your good eye," Snake said to Bad Eye. "What you be thinkin?"

"I be thinkin that the big crowd could have big advantages," Bad Eye replied.

"We ain't no good at pickpocketing," Billie said.

"Not thinking about that," said Bad Eye.

"Well," Jones said, "care to tell us what's on your mind?"

Bad Eye replied, "A giant crowd in downtown Harlan will

mean that stores outside the downtown area will be deserted. My mind just wondered to that nice little jewelry store in the Village Center Mall, I think it's called DiamondCraft. It's two or three miles from downtown. Won't be anybody there during the big downtown shindig. Could be real ripe for a robbery!"

Eagle Eye said, "Whoa, I done did one of those a few months back. The robbery went fine, but that damn Sheriff wound up with all the loot. Now that you mention it Bad Eye, that might not be such a bad idea. I certainly know how to hit one of those places.....and it sure could net us a lot of dough."

Bad Eye was smoking a cigar. He leaned back in his chair, blew a smoke-ring, got a big smile on his face, and said, "We'll put it together....we got about 3 weeks."

● ● ●

Prestonsburg, Kentucky

"Get in here," Big Jim yelled through the door to Mad Mike who was working on his car.

"Be right there," replied Mad Mike as he grabbed an old rag from his hip pocket and wiped his hands to get some of the oil and grease off.

"What's up?" Mad Mike said as he took a chair across the desk from Big Jim.

"I've learned more about our upcoming job in Lexington," Big Jim said.

"Oh," replied Mad Mike. "How does it look?"

Big Jim continued, "I been talking with our janitor snitch at that Dr. Peters' place at UK. His name is P Rat Cook. His real name is Paul Ratcliff Cook, but everyone calls him P Rat. He tells me that Peters is planning a fancy wine and cheese reception for the Carmen Twins on October 4th, and that it will be held in the area of his Center where the other three golden thingys are displayed. Since I learned that, I've been thinking how we could steal all five of them."

"Sounds like good thinking to me, Big Jim," said Mad Mike. "Exactly what do you have in mind?"

Big Jim replied, "I'm thinking of using sleeping gas. I've been talking with ole Mac Woolums. Mac worked at a military lab where they investigated different types of gases. After I told him what I was interested in, he said he could come up with canisters of some kind of sleeping gas that would knock out everyone in a room, but do no permanent harm. They'd just have a heck of a hangover. Then, after talking with P Rat he told me the dimensions of the room where the reception will be held, and after I passed that info to Mac he said he could put together two canisters of the gas that would put everyone in the room to sleep within about 30 seconds."

"How you going to deliver the gas?" asked Mad Mike.

"Got that all figured out," said Big Jim. "P Rat tells me that he's familiar with the air conditioning system for the room, and that he could place the canisters in the air ducts. I've got another guy that will put together a gizmo that can be attached to the canisters to open them by remote control. Once P Rat has them in the ducts and we're all set to go, I just press the button on the remote and everyone in the room is asleep within 30 seconds. We then just walk into the room and remove all five of the little golden thingys and then get the heck out of dodge. It should be a piece of cake."

"But how we gonna keep from going to sleep when we go in the room, Big Jim?" asked Mad Mike.

"Dumb ass! Even you should be able to figure that out. We wear gas masks, of course!", replied Big Jim.

"We ain't got no gas masks, Big Jim," Mad Mike replied.

"We'll have em," Big Jim said. "Mac Woolums will get what we need. Exactly one minute after we open them canisters we'll walk in the door with our gas masks on and grab those 5 golden thingys. It looks like the perfect crime to me."

"You real smart, Big Jim," replied Mad Mike.

"You right about that," said a smiling Big Jim.

● ● ●

Harlan County, Kentucky

Badass Brown sat in his old trailer not far from the community of Cawood, Kentucky in Harlan County. He had been brooding about his failures associated with Sheriff J. Bert Sterling. The acid contraption that he put together for Eagle Eye didn't work when he tried to use it to spray sulfuric acid onto the sheriff, and then the failure of ole Bennie to follow his instructions to embarrass the sheriff and others at the City Hall meeting. Badass did feel badly that Bennie had to spend several days in the hospital while his private parts recovered from the cat attack, but who could have known that the sheriff's vicious cat would be there. He was determined to do something to get even with the sheriff. And if by so doing he was able to turn a few bucks.....so much the better! His next plan had just arrived. The package sat before him on his coffee table. It was a drone.

Badass had been doing a lot of research on his computer learning about drones. He finally used his savings to order one that he thought would do the job. He planned to have the drone carry a grenade. His plan was to position the drone over the parking space reserved for Sheriff Sterling. He had been carefully following all the plans for the upcoming ACFes, and felt certain that the sheriff would at some point in time during the festival park the car in his reserved space, and hopefully have either the Carmen Twins or someone else with him that had possession of one or more of those golden anchor crosses. Just as they got out of his car Badass planned to drop the grenade from the drone. That should do in the sheriff and all that were with him, and he'd have ole Bennie ready to grab the anchor crosses and make a run for it. If it went as planned, he would take care of the sheriff and have one or more extremely valuable golden artifacts.

All he had to do between now and the festival was to learn how to fly the drone, and to put together a contraption to drop the grenade after pulling its pin. He was good at building such devices, so he didn't worry much about that, but he was less certain about learning how to fly the drone. Practice makes perfect, he thought.

•••

Paris, France

Renee Dubois, sitting at her desk at **Le Monde**, picked up her phone on the first ring and was rewarded by hearing the voice of Elisabeth Carmen, "Good morning Renee, I hope I didn't disturb you from your work."

"Not at all, Elisabeth, it's very good to hear your voice," replied Renee

"Likewise, my dear," said Elisabeth. "Henriette and I were just discussing our upcoming trip back to Kentucky, and I thought I'd check with you on the plans."

Renee replied, "My, my how time does fly. Our trip is now just a couple of weeks off. I am really getting excited about it. Our last trip was just super, and my editor was extremely pleased with the three stories I wrote while there. It seems our readers are most interested in following events about the anchor crosses."

"I'm pleased to know that," said Elisabeth. "We wondered if you would be able to be away for about a week? We were thinking of perhaps leaving on Tuesday, October 2nd and returning on Tuesday, October 9th. Do you think that would work for you?"

Renee looked at her calendar and then said, "I'll make it work, Elisabeth. I just can't thank you enough for your friendship and generous support. I do so much enjoy traveling and spending time with you two. You're a delight!"

"Thank you, my dear," Elisabeth said. "And we enjoy very much your company and expertise. Randy Peters has a reception scheduled for us on Thursday afternoon, October 4th. He wanted to invite several friends, a few politicians, a number of folks from his university as well as several members of the press to give them a private viewing of all the anchor crosses as well as time to talk with us. It sounded like fun. I hope you approve."

"Oh my, yes indeed.....I certainly do. It will be a great chance to gather more opinions for stories. Again, thank you so much," replied Renee.

Elisabeth continued, "And then Randy would drive us to Harlan on Friday morning for the festival, and then return to Lexington on Monday morning. We'd have time to rest up a bit before the return flight on Tuesday."

"Sounds delightful to me," said Renee. I assume I'll hear from your secretary regarding the specific flights, and I'll greatly look forward to it."

"You will, and so will we, my dear," said Elisabeth.

•••

Lexington, Kentucky

Randy Peters was exploding with anticipation. All plans for the upcoming visit of the Carmen Twins and Renee Dubois were set, and as far as he could determine the planning for the Anchor Cross Festival was right on schedule. He was greatly looking forward to all the activity. He felt certain that the results would be highly favorable to Harlan, to the Commonwealth of Kentucky, and to his institution, the University of Kentucky. Moreover, he thought the time everyone would spend together would have to further the understanding of the anchor crosses. Even though his research had been focused on them now for about 14 years, he knew that his knowledge about them barely scratched the surface. Anything new that he could uncover would be welcome indeed.

• • •

Harlan, Kentucky

Mayor Fred Knapp sat in his office at Creech Cafe thinking about all the planning for the ACFes. The committee had met several times, and it seemed that they had addressed all the needs required to make the festival a great success. There would be a few activities starting on Friday afternoon, October 5th, and there would be concluding activities on Sunday, October 7th, but the major activities would occur on

Saturday, October 6th. The Friday activity would be mostly vendors setting up, and generally getting ready for Saturday. A huge temporary stage would be constructed on the Harlan County Court House steps, and Saturday morning starting at 9 am a couple of music groups would play from there. Then at 10 am there would be a parade through the downtown area. The parade would conclude by 11 am, and at that time about a half dozen politicians would make brief talks from the court house stage. People would be encouraged to have lunch at one of the downtown restaurants, or from one of the many food vendors. The main program from the court house stage would start at 1 pm. Fred looked forward to being the master of ceremonies for this portion of the program. He would introduce the Governor, the Secretary for Economic Development, Dr. Randy Peters, and the Carmen Twins for brief talks. These talks should conclude by 3 pm. Following them on the stage would be a couple more music groups. The Seibert Anchor Cross Memorial, located on the Northwest corner of the Court House property, would be open all day, starting at 9 am and closing at 9 pm. Visitors could pass through the Memorial any time to view the Seibert, Pelle, and Helena anchor crosses. The Carmen Anchor Crosses would be worn by the twins until after they made their talks on the stage, and then they would be placed in the Memorial for viewing along with the other three. Sunday morning there would be a special church service at New Hope Baptist Church in which Pastor Raymond Bell would discuss the significance of the anchor crosses. All of those on the ACFes committee would be in attendance, as well as the Carmen Sisters. Activity from the court house stage would be limited to a couple more music groups on Sunday afternoon, and the Memorial would be open from 1 pm to 6 pm. Security was a major concern, and thanks to lots of support from the Governor the Kentucky State Police would provide a dozen troopers. Harlan City Police would add four more, and Sheriff Sterling had arranged to have three deputies from his Cumberland office as well as himself and Kyle on duty. So there would be a total of 21 law enforcement officers on duty during the festival. Six of these would be stationed at the Memorial at all times, two at the entrance, two inside, and two at the exit. The remaining officers would be assigned to control traffic, to be visible by walking through the crowd, or to be on or near the stage to assure that everything progressed in an orderly fashion.

Fred was tired, and decided he needed to leave his office and get a cup of coffee. He walked out of the office into the cafe, and was just about to pour his coffee when he heard a voice, "There you are, Fred. Would you please come over here a moment?"

The voice belonged to Mrs. Harrison. Fred replied, "Oh, hi Mrs. Harrison. Sure, I'll be right there." And he started walking toward her.

She was standing beside a wall looking intently at a photograph that Fred had posted. "Would you please tell me what this is all about?"

Fred saw the picture she was interested in, and said, "Yeah, that does look a bit strange, doesn't it?"

The picture was of a man standing beside an unusual looking bed.

Fred continued, "Well, the story that goes with that picture is something like this. That guy had a fear that someone was hiding under his bed at night, so he finally decided to go see a shrink. He told him, 'Doc, I've got a problem. Every time I go to bed I think there's somebody under it. I'm scared, and I think I'm going crazy.' The shrink said, 'Just put yourself in my hands for one year. Come talk to me three times a week and we should be able to get rid of those fears.' The man then asked, 'How much do you charge?' The doctor replied, 'Eighty dollars per visit.' The man said, 'I'll sleep on it.' Six months later the doctor met the man on the street and said, 'Why didn't you come to see me about those fears you were having?' The man replied, 'Well, eighty bucks a visit, three times a week for a year, is $12,480. A bartender cured me for $10. I was so happy to have saved all that money I went out and bought me a new pickup truck.' The shrink said with a bit of an attitude, 'Is that so? And how, may I ask, did the bartender cure you?' The man replied, 'He told me to cut the legs off the bed.....ain't nobody under there now!'"

Mrs. Harrison started to giggle, and said, "Goes to prove, just forget the shrinks, have a drink, and talk with the bartender!"

Fred laughed, and said, "You got it. It's always good to get a second opinion!"

Chapter 16

Prestonsburg, Kentucky

Big Jim Owens, Mad Mike Hatfield, P Rat Cook, and Mac Woolums were all huddled around a card table set up in the middle of Big Jim's office in the back of his gas station. It was Sunday, September 30th. P Rat and Mac didn't have to work on weekends, so they were able to comply with Big Jim's summons for them to meet. All were looking intently at the two shinny canisters lying on the card table. Each had a strange looking apparatus attached to their valve.

Big Jim spoke, "Okay Mac, they look pretty.....I guess, and now you're going to demonstrate how they work?"

Mac Woolums had a confident smile as he replied, "Absolutely Big Jim! For purposes of this demonstration I've filled the canisters with compressed air containing a red dye, so we'll be able to see it escape. A lot of the money you're going to pay me for putting these together went to locate the remotely controlled actuators that open the valves. And then I had to modify the valves themselves so that when the actuators get a signal from the remote control to open, they simply pull off a seal on the valves. The valves themselves are always left in the open position. So when this happens, all the gas in the canisters is immediately released. Does that make sense?"

Big Jim, Mad Mike, and P Rat all looked a bit puzzled at Mac. Mad Mike and P Rat nodded slowly like they might have understood, and Big Jim said, "I'm not sure I understood all that technical stuff, but it sounded like you knew what you were doing. All we care about is that it works. And you're getting ready to demonstrate that right now."

"Right-O," Mac replied. "I had to have two remotes, one for each canister. I couldn't get two of the actuators that operated on the same frequency that would let us just have one remote to operate both canisters, so you'll have to press buttons on two remotes to release all the gas. And that's good for this demonstration, since I'll be able to activate each canister separately to demonstrate their reliability."

Big Jim, Mad Mike, and P Rat just had blank stares on their faces, and Big Jim said, "Just get on with it Mac. Show us that they work."

"Okay, okay," Mac responded. "I just wanted to make sure you understood."

Mac then picked up one of the remote controls and said, "Now you see this red button right here?" as he pointed to the button, "You just need to press it down and hold it for about 1 second. When that's done you'll see the actuator on that canister move," and he pointed toward one of the canisters. "That opens the sealed valve, and then you'll see the red colored air flowing out. It'll all take place quickly."

"Show us," said Big Jim.

"Watch," Mac said as he pressed the red button. All then went exactly as Mac had said it would. Red air came streaming out of the canister and quickly tinted all the air in the room.

"Worked like a charm," Big Jim replied. "Now let's try #2."

Mac reached for the other remote, and handed it to Big Jim and said, "You do the honors this time, Big Jim."

Big Jim smiled as he took the remote and pressed it's red button. Again, the actuator moved to open the seal and red colored air rushed out of the canister.

"Slick as a ribbon!" said Mad Mike.

Mac beamed with pride.

"Yeah, I'm satisfied, Mac. You done good! All you need to do now is load them things with the sleeping gas and get em all ready to go again. We'll just have to be real careful not to press those red buttons by accident."

Mad Mike replied, "Yeah, we'd better not play with em in the car driving to Lexington. If one went off by accident the results wouldn't be pretty."

"You got that right," said Mac.

"So," Big Jim said, "now that everything's set with the sleeping gas, lets talk about the room where the party will be held. P Rat here's got all the details to show us."

After Mac removed the canisters off the table, P Rat

spread a sheet of paper that was the floor plan of the room where the reception was to be held. Each of the four men held one corner of the sheet, and P Rat said, "Okay guys, this is the layout. As you can see, the room is about 40 feet long by about 30 feet wide. The Seibert, Pelle, and Helena Anchor Crosses are in display cases located here along this wall. My understanding from overhearing Dr. Peters discuss the upcoming reception with his secretary, is that the Carmen Twins will be wearing their anchor crosses. The other three in the display cases will be available for attendees to actually touch and examine, so the thick plexiglass lids on them will be open. That's lucky for you, because if they were shut and locked they would be virtually impossible to open. The door that you'll be entering through is located right here. I'll place the canisters in the air conditioning ventilation ducts, located in these areas. I'll make sure that the fans for the air conditioners are continuously circulating air. So you'll just park in the Center's parking lot, located right here off Rose Street, and then when you're ready to go you stand beside this door, press the remote controls, wait about 1 minute, and then open the door and enter. By that time everyone should be out cold, including the security guards. Questions?"

Big Jim replied, "Are we certain the door will be open? Is it the same door that all the guests will be using?"

"Yes," replied P Rat. "It is an outside door, and normally is locked securely. But for this reception it's the most convenient way for folks to enter, so it'll definitely be unlocked."

Big Jim got a huge smile on his face and said, "I think everything is good to go. Just as soon as we pull this thing off, I'll pay you guys our agreed upon amount, and we should all be on easy street. The gold in those five thingys will be worth well over half a million. So just as soon as I get them melted down we'll have our money. No problem at all in selling gold."

The other three grinned. Mad Mike started rubbing his hands together. P Rat and Mac nodded their heads in agreement. The time for their heist was now only 4 days off!

Chapter 17

Knoxville, Tennessee

The junkyard gang was out in back of their office building rehearsing their upcoming robbery of the DiamondCraft jewelry store in Harlan on October 6th.

Bad Eye had taken a stick and drawn in the dirt a huge outline of what he said was representative of the floor plan for the small mall where the store was located. Since all five of them were from Harlan, they were very familiar with the mall and its approximate dimensions. Just outside the door to the mall entrance Bad Eye had drawn the outline of their car parked at the curb.

"Now, let's go over it one more time," Bad Eye said. "I know you're getting tired of all this, but practice makes perfect, and we do want to pull this off perfectly."

He took his stick and pointed to the outline of their car, and said, "So first we drive up to the curb....right here. I'm driving, and will stay with the car, since with this patch over my eye I'd be recognized immediately by anyone that might see us. You four will immediately jump out of the car wearing your disguises and go into the mall. Since about everyone in Harlan will be downtown at the shindig, you likely won't encounter many people at all in the mall. If you do, just nod politely and go on....they won't think anything about you. When you get to the DiamondCraft, right here, Jones will stop and play lookout. If a customer comes to the store Jones can tell them it's closed due to a plumbing problem. The other three of you will go into the store. Once inside, Eagle Eye will yell, 'Everyone freeze....lay down on the floor, NOW'. And you'll all wave your guns so everyone can see them. There should only be three employees at most in the store. There could be one or two customers, but not likely. Once you're sure they're all doing as told, then Billie, Snake, and Eagle Eye will fill the bags they'll be carrying with all the good stuff in the display cases. The cases won't be locked, since this will be during normal business hours. You got to move fast. Then when you've got all the loot, come running out of the store to the car. They key to the whole operation is to do it within 10 minutes max."

Bad Eye continued, "So, everyone in position, and let's go through it."

All five then moved to stand within the outline in the dirt that Bad Eye had drawn to represent their car. Then at Bad Eye's command, the four moved from the 'car' into the store. They moved down the mall corridor to the jewelry store. Jones stayed at the door, the other three entered the store. 'Everyone freeze....lay down on the floor, NOW', Bad Eye could hear Eagle Eye shout. Then the three went through the motions of moving about the store to gather the jewelry. Then all four came running back out, and stepped back into the outline drawn to represent the car.

"That took six minutes," said Bad Eye, looking at his watch. "No doubt the real thing'll take a little longer since we have to physically open the cases and get the loot out into our bags, but it shouldn't take more than another 4 minutes. So I say we're pretty close. We'll practice another few times before the big show on Saturday."

"Is that really necessary, Bad Eye?" asked Billie.

"Yes, it is," replied Bad Eye. "And we've got one more job to do before Saturday. I want Jones to drive to Harlan and pay a visit to the DiamondCraft. He needs to case the store to locate all the good stuff. Jones, you can tell the clerk that you just want to look around.....that you're interested in buying a gift for a friend, but you don't have anything in mind. After you've said that you should be free to wander around. We want to know exactly where all the good stuff is located, so we won't waste time loading our bags with junk. You'll need to carefully remember the cases with good stuff, and then immediately when you come out of the store make a sketch showing the cases that we need to hit. That'll save us a bunch of time."

"When you want me to go, Bad Eye?" asked Jones.

"Leave first thing in the morning," replied Bad Eye. "Once you get back we'll know which cases we want to hit, and we can better rehearse another time or two before Saturday."

Eagle Eye spoke up with a grin on his face, "Bad Eye, I hope it don't rain between now and Saturday, or else your nice drawing here in the dirt might get washed out!"

Bad Eye said with a grin, "Don't worry Eagle Eye, I've got it all memorized. I can reproduce this drawing in a flash. I think we're just about all set to make a nice hit."

Chapter 18

Harlan County, Kentucky

Fatso Chapel heard the door open and looked up from reading his novel to see Sheriff Sterling entering Maggard's grocery.

"Another visit?" asked Fatso. "You keep coming here sheriff and its going to give us a bad reputation!"

Bert smiled at Fatso and said, "Strictly business, Fatso, strictly business. I need to see Trigger. Can you please press the button to let me in his office."

"Of course I can," Fatso replied. "But first, can you tell me what's black and white and red all over?"

"That's an easy and old one Fatso," Bert responded. "A newspaper is black and white and read all over."

"Wrong!" replied Fatso. "A zebra with a sunburn is black and white and red all over!"

Fatso pressed the button that released the lock on Triggers office, and the sheriff opened the door and walked in.

"Morning Bert, thank you for coming over," said Trigger as he got up from his desk and walked around to shake hands with the sheriff.

Bert replied, "Well, I'm always a little concerned when I get a call from you wanting to talk, so I thought I'd better head over here."

Bert pulled up a chair as Trigger went back and seated himself at his desk.

"It's probably nothing, sheriff," Trigger replied, "but you told me earlier that if I heard anything that sounded suspicious regarding your upcoming Anchor Cross Festival you'd appreciate me sharing it with you. I know the festival is this coming weekend, and I had a conversation yesterday with C.G. Howard that I thought I should probably share with you."

"I'm all ears, Trigger," Bert said.

Trigger then said, "As you know, C.G. works at the trade school. He teaches machine shop. C.G. and Badass Brown grew up and went to school at Harlan together. They've maintained a friendship over the years. I was having lunch at McDonalds yesterday and C.G. walked in and sat down with me. We talked about a lot of different things, but got to talking about all those drones that you see on the news these days. Then he told me that his friend Badass Brown had purchased a drone, and had come to him to get a special gizmo built."

"What kind of gizmo," asked the sheriff.

"I'm not exactly sure," replied Trigger, "but as best I could understand from what C.G. said it was some kind of contraption that would hold a baseball. When the thing was activated it slid open to release the baseball and at the same time pulled a string. C.G. said Badass told him that he wanted to use his drone to carry the contraption over a little league baseball game and drop the baseball and at the same time pull a string that released a banner that said 'GO HARLAN'. That just didn't make a lot of sense to me. I know you and ole Badass have had some problems lately, so I just had the feeling that I should at least bring this to your attention. It's likely not anything, but it did sound like he's up to something, and being right before the festival weekend I thought I'd better give you a head's up."

Bert got a frown on his face, and said, "That does sound a bit strange. And I agree with you that it sounds like Badass is up to something. Unfortunately, nothing you've told me is illegal, so I don't know anything I can do until he actually breaks the law. But I sure do appreciate your sharing it with me. I'll pass the story along to Kyle and my other deputies, and have them be especially alert to watch for drones. You certainly don't see many of those here in Harlan County."

"Just trying to do my civic duty, sheriff," Trigger replied as he stood to see Bert out of his office. "If I hear anything further on it I'll be sure to give you a call."

"Thanks, Trigger, I do appreciate you," Bert replied as he left Trigger's office and entered again into the grocery.

"Hope you guys had a good visit," Fatso shouted to Bert as he walked toward the grocery store door. "One more question.....you know what you call a camel without a hump?"

Bert was silent, and kept walking.

"Humphrey," Fatso said with a giggle.

Bert slammed the door on his way out.

●●●

Badass Brown sat in his trailer holding the drone with the assembled mechanism he had gotten from C.G. Howard. Badass felt a little bad having to tell C.G. all those lies about what the mechanism was for, but he really didn't have a choice. He certainly wasn't going to tell him it would be used to drop a grenade on the sheriff. The time was getting close, and he still had to field test the device before Saturday. He had been very fortunate to be able to locate a grenade. He had a buddy that was in the national guard, and was in charge of equipment and munitions. He had paid him $200 for the grenade. It was a 'timed fuse' type of grenade. There was a pin that held the safety lever. Once the pin was pulled and the lever released, the grenade exploded 5 seconds later. The mechanism he got from C.G. had a slider that the grenade rested on. When ready to be dropped, a remote control activated the mechanism to open the slider and at the same time pulled the pin from the grenade. The safety lever was released when the grenade dropped through the slider opening. Five seconds later the grenade would explode. But Badass needed to test it. He had spent many hours learning how to fly the drone. He had located a remote area in the mountains about a mile from his trailer that was suitable to practice flying the drone and not be seen by anyone. The challenge had been to come up with a mock grenade to use for the final test flight. He had spent the last week working on a wooden model that had all the elements of the grenade, and he would use it for the final test.

Well, it was time to do the test. He gathered up the drone with the mechanism attached, and with the mock grenade positioned on its slider. He put the assembly in a special wooden box he had constructed just to house the drone, got the remote control, and then started the one mile walk to the test area.

After about a half hour walk he finally arrived at the test location. He sat the box and remote down and then carefully looked around to see if he was all alone. Satisfied that there was no one to watch the test but himself, he opened the box and removed the drone assembly. Power for the drone was supplied by a rechargeable battery, and he had been careful to make sure it was fully charged. Badass had previously taken two straight tree limbs, each about 6 feet long, and after stripping off all their branches had laid them on the ground one over the other, forming an 'X'. That was to be the mock target, i.e. the sheriffs car.

Using the drone's remote control he turned on the power. The propellers responded as the drone sprang to life. He guided it upward, and then flew it around the area just to get a little more flying practice. He stood about 200 feet away from the 'X' marked by the crossed tree limbs, and maneuvered the drone to an altitude of about 500 feet above the mock target. He then let it hover there for a bit. The electric motors and propellers were quiet enough that he could hardly hear it. He felt certain that with all the racket that would be coming from the festival on Saturday that no one would hear his drone.

The moment had come.   Time to release the mock grenade. He looked at the red button on the mechanism remote control that C.G. had furnished him. He pressed the button, and looked toward the bottom of the drone. He saw the actuator move to pull the pin from the wooden grenade, and then the slider opened to drop the grenade. He then watched it fall the 500 feet toward the target and landed only about 8 feet from the center of the 'X'!

Badass got a big grin on his face as he shouted, "BOOM! Sheriff, you're a goner!"

• • •

As Bert walked into Creech's Cafe he reached up and gave Polly a stroke and said, "Bird, you're looking well today."

Polly responded, "Howdy sheriff, howdy sheriff."

He looked around the cafe and spotted his deputy and the mayor sitting at a table toward the back. He proceeded there to join them.

As Bert took a seat Kyle said, "How'd the visit with Trigger go?"

Bert explained what Trigger had told him regarding Badass and the drone.

"Don't see many of them things around Harlan," replied the mayor. "But I guess we should keep on the look-out for one now."

"I can't think of how he could cause a problem with one, but it never hurts to be cautious," Bert said.

Mayor Knapp then said, "Boys, I'm really getting nervous. Here we are just a few days from the ACFes and I just don't know if we've got all our bases covered or not. People just don't realize how much work goes into one of these things. I do know we're going to have a really good crowd. I understand that all the motels in Harlan, Pineville, Middlesboro, and even as far as Barbourville and Corbin are full up for the weekend. Likely be the biggest crowd our little town has ever hosted."

Bert replied, "Now mayor, you've got everything under control. I'm sure that by this time next week we'll be sitting here talking about what a big success it was. Don't worry about it!"

"I just naturally worry," said Fred. "Can't help it."

"You worry too much and it'll cause you to get sick, Fred," cautioned Kyle.

"I don't think I worry that much," Fred said. "But that does remind me of the story that goes with that picture up there on the wall." Fred pointed to a picture of a very elderly man eating what looked to be a cookie. Bert and Kyle looked at the picture, and Bert said with a grin, "I bet you're going to tell us about that cookie he's eating."

Fred Started, "That old man is 96 years old. He was in his

bed about to take his last breath when he suddenly smelled the fresh aroma of his favorite chocolate-chip cookies wafting up the stairs. He gathered his remaining strength and managed to lift out of bed. He grabbed his walker and started making his way toward the stairs. He very cautiously and slowly made his way down the stairs, and finally into the kitchen. Were it not for death's agony at his doorstep, he would have thought himself already in heaven. There, spread out on waxed-paper on the kitchen table were literally hundreds of his favorite chocolate-chip cookies. Was it truly heaven, or was it one final act of love from his devoted wife....seeing to it that he left this world a happy man? Mustering one great final effort, he threw himself toward the table, landing on his knees in a rumpled posture. His parched lips parted. He could almost taste the cookie already in his mouth, seemingly bringing him back to life. His aged and withered hand trembled on its way to a cookie at the edge of the table, when it was suddenly slapped by his wife, who then said, 'Stay out of those, they're for the funeral.'"

All three were laughing so hard that tears formed. Then Kyle said, "Well, she must have let him have one at least, since he looks to be happily eating one in that picture."

"Yeah," Fred replied. "I think that cookie and the smell kept him going for quite a bit longer."

Bert and Kyle stood, and Bert said, "Fred, thanks for the coffee and the story. Try and not worry about the festival. Everything will be just fine. You take care."

Bert and Kyle headed back to work.

Chapter 19

Lexington, Kentucky

Randy Peters was sitting in his office on Monday morning, October 1. His intercom phone buzzed and he said, "Yes Joyce."

"Elisabeth Carmen is on line 1 for you Dr. Peters."

"Thanks Joyce, I'll get it," and Randy switched to line 1.

"Well, well, good morning, or I guess I should say good afternoon, Elisabeth. How's everything in Madrid?"

"Good morning to you, Randy. And yes, it's almost 4 pm here in Madrid. I hope you are doing well," Elisabeth said.

"Yes, just fine, thanks," Randy replied. "Just looking forward with great anticipation to seeing you, Henriette, and Renee tomorrow. I hope the trip is all on schedule, and that everyone is well."

"We're all very excited. We've got our luggage all packed and looking forward to seeing you and visiting again in beautiful Kentucky. But I did have a favor to ask of you," Elisabeth said.

"Anything at all," replied Randy.

Elisabeth then said, "I don't know if you recall, but during your visit here you might have met Harry Kalos. Harry is my chief of security, and he usually hangs out down at the main gate. When Julien drove you here from the airport you may have seen Harry when you passed through our gate."

Randy said, "Yes, I do recall seeing him, and I remember Julien speaking to him as we entered."

Elisabeth continued, "Well, and this is a little embarrassing for me to ask, but a couple of things presented themselves that prompted me to make this call. Harry is an extremely dedicated and hard working guy. He has been with our family now for about 20 years. He watches after Henriette and me day in and day out, and we have great difficulty in getting him to take any time off. He hasn't taken a vacation for over 5 years now. That was one thing. The other was that Henriette and I have been discussing the fact that there may be security concerns associated with displaying the valuable anchor crosses. I think I do recall a couple of serious instances that occurred in the past with the other anchor crosses that involved potential thieves. So, having said that, what I'm leading up to is to ask if it would work for you if we brought Harry along with us on the trip. It would give him a little break and some time off from his usual routine, and he would be available for security duty....and, I might add, he is very good."

Randy replied, "Oh, that would work great. I don't know

why you were hesitant to ask. He would be most welcome, and his presence would certainly help with the security aspects. One question, it seems to me that I recall when I saw him he did not look nearly as large as most security people. Am I remembering correctly?"

"Your memory serves you well," Elisabeth replied. "Harry is only about 5 feet 6 inches, and weighs only about 175 pounds. But every pound is solid muscle. He works out all the time, and runs 5 miles daily. He's in super shape, plus he has black belts, or whatever they're called, from various martial arts schools. My sister and I have had many encounters with unfriendly people during Harry's 20 years with us and I can assure you Harry won every encounter very easily. Don't let his size fool you, he can more than take care of himself and us as well!"

"That's good to know," Randy said. "I'll make sure not to challenge him to hand wrestling! The only logistical problem that comes to mind is his sleeping arrangement while at my house. As you know, I have a four bedroom home. But I do have a very comfortable sleeper-sofa in my den, which serves as an extra bedroom when needed, and there is a bathroom just off from it. Do you think he would object to using it?"

"That would be just perfect for him," Elisabeth responded. "I know he would not object at all. Thank you so much for understanding. He'll be extra excited when I tell him we want him along with us. It will do him a world of good, and his presence will certainly mean added security."

"Great," Randy replied. "Sounds like everything is good to go. I'll look forward to seeing all of you at Bluegrass Field tomorrow. My understanding is that you three will meet up with Renee in Atlanta and then be on the same flight on to Lexington."

"That's correct," Elisabeth said. "See you tomorrow!"

Chapter 20

Lexington, Kentucky

The Carmen sisters, Renee, and Harry arrived on schedule Tuesday evening. Randy gathered the tired group and took them to his home for a well deserved rest. Wednesday was spent mostly recovering from the Tuesday trip, but all did go to the University of Kentucky that afternoon to visit with Randy at the Center for Appalachian Research and to make plans for the reception that was scheduled for Thursday afternoon.

•••

Big Jim Owens and Mad Mike Hatfield had driven from Prestonsburg to Lexington on Wednesday afternoon. The two had just gotten back to their motel room after eating a large dinner at the Cracker Barrel. It was about 8 pm when they heard a knock on their door.

As he lay stretched out on one of the beds Big Jim shouted, "Come on in, its unlocked", and in walked P Rat Cook.

P Rat looked at the two of them, each stretched out on a bed, and said, "You two look like you're ready for bed.....I thought we were going to go over the plans for tomorrow."

"Just letting our food digest, P Rat," replied Mad Mike.

"Yeah, can't get in a big hurry on these things," Big Jim said.

The two slowly raised up from their supine positions and walked over to the small table and sat. P Rat joined them.

"You get the gas canisters here okay?" asked P Rat.

Big Jim reached down and grabbed an attaché case, placed it on the table, and then opened it as he said, "Got those babies right here."

"They look wicked," P Rat replied. "You sure they're all ready to go?"

"Mac Woolums assured us they are loaded with the sleeping gas, and all set to release it when the red buttons here on the two remotes are pressed," said Mad Mike.

"I hope he knows what he's doing," P Rat responded.

"He does," Big Jim said. "So let's talk now about the plans. My understanding is that you are going to put one of these canisters in each of two air ducts in the room where the reception is to be held. When are you going to do that?"

P Rat said, "I normally get to work very early, usually about 7 am. But tomorrow I'll get there around 6 am, and place the canisters in the ducts. I've already carefully checked them.

I took a ladder in there a couple of days ago and told the people I had to vacuum the dust out. That gave me a chance to take the screws out of the vents and remove them to look inside. There was plenty of room inside the ducts for the canisters. It won't take me more than 5 minutes to put them in place tomorrow morning. There's never anyone around at that hour of the morning, so I should be able to just carry them in and get them in place without being noticed."

"Good," replied Big Jim. "And then sometime before the reception you're going to set the fans to operate continuously, right?"

"No problem at all," P Rat said. "I know just where the fan switch is. I'll set it to 'continuous' operation sometime during my lunch break. Then, when you hit those red buttons the air moving through the duct system will deliver the sleeping gas just like you want."

Big Jim then said, "Okay, so I understand the reception is set to begin at 3 pm. We'll pull up and park in the lot beside the Center at exactly 3:15 pm. That way anyone running a little late should be there, and we shouldn't run into anyone outside. We'll sit in our car for about 5 minutes just looking to make sure everything looks good, and then we'll get out and walk over to the door going into the center. We'll be dressed to look like janitors, and will be carrying our gas masks in a black plastic bag. If anyone should spot us, we won't look suspicious. Mad Mike will carry the bag, and I'll be carrying the two remote controls. When we get to the door I'll press the red buttons on each of the remotes to trigger the canisters to start releasing the sleeping gas. Then we'll take the next minute putting on our gas masks. Then we'll open the door and rush in. Everyone in the room should be out cold and lying on the floor. Then we'll just gather the five gold thingys, three from their display cases and the other two from around the necks of the Carmen sisters, place them in the black trash bag, and then head for the car. We should be able to do all that in no more than 5 minutes. Once back in the car we'll head for Prestonsburg. The sleeping gas should keep all those people out for at least an hour, according to Mac. By the time they wake up we'll be half way home. Should work slick as snot on a doorknob."

P Rat said, "Sounds like everything is all set. My shift ends at 3:30, so I'll take off then, so no one should suspect me of anything. I'll look forward to getting my cut just as soon as you melt the thingys and get the gold sold, Big Jim."

"Don't worry about getting your money. You'll get it," replied Big Jim.

Mad Mike then said, "Well, it seems to me that by this time tomorrow we'll all be rich. So why don't we just get a good night's rest and be all ready for tomorrow's heist."

All nodded approval, with big smiles. P Rat departed and Big Jim and Mad Mike went to bed.

Chapter 21

Harlan, Kentucky

Bennie, the town drunk, and Badass Brown sat in the back of Badass's old van. It was parked directly across from the Harlan County Court House, in front of Creech Cafe. Several months ago Badass had painted the old van. He had a couple of gallons of dark blue paint and he used it to paint the van with a 4" brush. It didn't look the greatest, but was a big improvement over the old faded white paint with the "Bunny Bread" signs still visible on its sides. At least no one would recognize it as his old van, and it seemed to fit in nicely with all the construction going on over at the court house to build the stage and with all the other concession vans and trucks parked around in preparation for the festival. It was now Thursday morning, and ACFes began tomorrow, with all the major events on Saturday.

Badass said, "Now Bennie, do you think you know exactly what you are to do?"

"You think I'm stupid?" Bennie replied. "I'm not, and right now I'm even sober. So, yeah, I understand exactly what you want me to do."

"Didn't mean to insult you, Bennie, just trying to make sure we've got all our bases covered," Badass said. "If all goes according to plan you'll have enough money after Saturday to move up from drinking that cheap stuff to Jack Daniels, with a lot left over. Think about that!"

Bennie replied with a big smile on his face, "Yeah, I been thinking about that. Been thinking about that a lot."

"So," Badass said, "just listen closely one more time as I tell you what we're going to do. I know you think you already know, but let's go over it one more time."

"Okay," replied Bennie.

Badass continued, "Saturday morning will kick off with some activities on the stage over there, followed by a parade through town. The big event will be after lunch, starting at 1 pm. From what I've learned, several of the honored guests will have lunch back at Pastor Bell's house following the morning parade. After they finish their lunch I figure that the sheriff will drive the Carmen sisters wearing their golden anchor crosses back to the court house for the afternoon ceremony. He'll likely park in his reserved parking spot there beside the court house sometime around 12:45. You'll be just behind the court house with my drone. You'll be just around the corner of the court house, so that the sheriff would not spot you when he pulls into his parking place. But you'll be peeking around the corner to look for his arrival. When you see his car coming you will call me on the cell phone I will give you. When I get your call I'll know it's time to turn on the drone. You'll have positioned it on the ground in the back of the court house where we scouted out. No one should see it sitting there. You'll then see the propellers start to turn and it will start to rise. Make real sure you're not standing close to it. Once it gets a little altitude I'll be able to spot it from sitting in the driver's seat of my van and looking out the window. If anyone sees me working the remote control they'll just think I'm working on something for the van or for the ceremony..... they won't connect me with the drone. I'll then maneuver the drone to a position above the sheriff's car after he parks it. I can clearly see his parking space from here. I'll have the drone up high enough that the sheriff won't see or hear it. Then, just as Bert and the Carmen sisters get out of the car I'll press the button here on the remote that releases the grenade. Make sure that you're back around the corner and behind the court house when you see that grenade start to drop. The next thing you'll hear will be the explosion of the grenade. When you hear that, you run quickly and jerk those golden anchor crosses from the Carmen sisters and then run with them real quickly back behind the court house and then just walk calmly back to your house. I'll then drive the van to your house while everyone is concerned with the commotion caused by the explosion. Then we'll figure out how to sell those things for as much money as we can get for them. You got all that?"

"Yeah, but a couple of things still bother me," Bennie

replied. "After that grenade goes off there's going to be all kinds of blood and stuff everywhere. It's going to be real messy for me to try and get those anchor crosses off the Carmen sisters. And I still don't know if I can do it before people get there."

"Timing is everything, Bennie," Badass said. "Bert and the Carmen sisters will be dead. You just need to run fast and just rip those crosses from their necks. And then run fast back behind the court house. All the crowd will be in the front of the court house, and the big stage will be blocking their view toward the side where the sheriff will park. They'll hear the explosion, but will likely just think it's fireworks or something associated with the ceremony. I feel certain you'll have enough time to grab those crosses and get gone before anyone comes over there. Just think about all the Jack Daniels you'll have after this is all over. That should motivate you to move real quickly!"

"I guess," Bennie said with hesitation. "I just hope you're right."

"Of course I'm right," Badass replied. "It'll work like a charm. Now you remember that you need to come here to the van right at noon on Saturday and knock three times on the back door. I'll open it and you can come in and pick up the drone all ready to go. It'll be all nicely placed in a little cloth bag. Then you can just carry it to the back of the court house and place it where I told you. The cell phone will also be in the bag, so after the drone's in place you just watch for the sheriff to arrive around 12:45 and give me a call as soon as you see his car approaching. Everything will go smoothly. I'll be waiting to hear you knock on the van's back door around noon. You won't let me down, will you?"

"Three knocks," Bennie said. "Three knocks at noon."

Bennie then headed home to have a little snort. Badass was worried about Bennie's role in his plan, but thought he had him sufficiently motivated. If he just showed up at noon on Saturday, and was reasonably sober, it should work. But Badass wasn't taking any chances this time. He was tired of failing at doing in the sheriff. He looked over at the rifle mounted in the rack on the inside wall of his van. If for any reason Bennie, the drone, or the grenade failed, he would then go to plan B, which was to wait until the ceremony was underway and he had a good clear shot from the van at the sheriff on the stage. Eagle Eye Looney had modified Badass's van previously when he tried in a failed attempt to shoot the sheriff during another ceremony on the court house stage about a year ago. Eagle Eye had drilled a hole in the side of the van such that a rifle barrel could fit through and be pointed toward the court house. The hole was high enough that people outside wouldn't notice it, but Badass could stand up in the van and perfectly position the rifle to point toward the court house stage. If plan A failed, then plan B would be for Badass to use the rifle to shoot the sheriff, in which case the noise from the gunshot should be almost totally muffled by the walls of the van and Badass would be able to just wait until the coast was clear and drive off in his van. Plan B would yield no money, but a lot of satisfaction. Badass still held out hope for a successful Plan A. That would yield both satisfaction and money. He had a big smile on his face as he locked up his old van and started walking to his old beat-up car. The next time he would be back at his van would be Saturday morning, and he was getting excited already!

Chapter 22

Lexington, Kentucky

Rat Cook arrived at work just after 6 am on Thursday morning. He carried an attaché. He noticed no one else at the early hour, and upon entering the Center proceeded immediately to the room where the reception was to be held that afternoon. He got the ladder and climbed up to remove the grill over one of the air ducts in the room. He then climbed down and opened the attaché and carefully removed one of the two canisters. He knew it contained the sleeping gas, and got a bit spooked just thinking about it. He then slowly climbed the ladder holding the canister and placed it in the air duct. After going back down the ladder he grabbed the grill and then climbed back up and secured the grill in place with its screws. Then he repeated the procedure with the other air duct, placing the second sleeping gas canister in position. He then stored the ladder and took the attaché and placed it in his janitors closet. Everything was all set. All he had to do now was to go about his normal duties for the day, and to make sure he was nowhere near the reception room starting at about 3 pm. When he left for the day at 3:30 pm everyone in the reception room should be sound asleep and Big Jim and Mad Mike should be well on their way back to Prestonsburg with all 5 of the golden anchor crosses. At least that was the plan.

•••

The Carmen sisters, Renee Dubois, and Harry Kalos had all recovered nicely from their trip. Randy had really enjoyed hosting them at his home, and he had especially found Harry to be most interesting. In his discussions with him he had learned that Harry's parents were from Greece, but had moved to Madrid when he was only a young child. Harry had excelled in school and had completed a two year course at a local college that resulted in his having received an associate degree in business. He was only 20 years old at the time, and after working a couple of years for a bank decided he wanted to get into security work. He was fortunate to have a friend that worked for a large security firm, and his friend's recommendation got him a job there. Fortunately for Harry, his first and final assignment with the security firm involved working for the Carmen sisters. He became so well liked by them that after two years they talked him into leaving the security firm to head up security at their estate. He had now been with them for approximately 20 years. He was a fitness nut. He spent hours each day working out, including a 5 mile daily run. He had taken courses in karate since he was a teenager, and had earned the black belt. While only about 175 pounds and 5 feet, 6 inches tall, he was an extremely powerful man. Randy found him to also be a very good man, and extremely pleasant. He had greatly enjoyed getting to know Harry over the past couple of days.

The five of them arrived at the Center for Appalachian Research around 9 am on Thursday morning. Randy normally got to his office by 7 am, but he didn't want to get his guests up that early, knowing they would have a busy and tiring day. As the entourage walked into the Center they met P Rat walking outside for a smoke.

"Good morning P Rat," Randy greeted as they passed in the hall.

"Morning Dr. Peters," P Rat replied as he continued walking.

Each of the five exchanged greetings with Randy's secretary, Joyce, as they entered into his office. After being seated, Joyce entered with a tray of coffee and snacks.

Randy said with a grin, "Thank you Joyce, fortified with that caffeine and sugar I think we'll likely make it through the day."

Joyce smiled as she left the office and closed the door.

As each grabbed a cup of coffee and sweet roll Randy said, "I do hope you folks don't mind terribly to help me with this reception today. I just thought it was a great opportunity for me to share both the new anchor crosses and yourselves with a number of my friends and colleagues, as well as with the governor and our economic secretary. I just hope it won't be too boring and tiring for you."

Renee then spoke, "Well, speaking for myself, I greatly appreciate your setting up the reception. To meet these people will be super for me, and will help provide new material for my next articles. I'm excited about the reception!"

Elisabeth spoke next, "I agree totally with Renee. We are here to show our beautiful anchor crosses. The folks that will be at the reception are the kind of people who will appreciate them and spread our story. Henriette and I are most excited about the reception, and we too thank you for going to all the trouble to host it."

Finally Harry said, "It's an opportunity for me to be able to work a little! I can keep a good sharp eye on all those anchor crosses, and hopefully be of help if anything should go wrong."

Randy replied, "Thank each of you for those encouraging remarks. I do sincerely think that the people you'll meet this afternoon will be interesting. I know that each of them will certainly enjoy meeting and talking with you."

• • •

Joyce and a couple of assistants at the Center had done a great job of setting up the room for the reception. The display cases containing the three resident anchor crosses had been opened to allow the guests to remove them for close examination. Lemonade and cookies had been placed on a table near the entrance to the room. A dais and lectern with a microphone had been set up in the far end of the room for Randy's remarks. Everything seemed to be ready. It was 2:30 pm when Randy, the Carmen sisters, Renee, and Harry walked into the reception room.

"The governor and his economic secretary should be arriving at about 2:45 pm," Randy said. "Hopefully they'll get here before most of the other guests, and that'll give you a little extra time to talk with them."

Randy had no more than finished saying this when the outside door opened and in walked a Kentucky State trooper followed by Governor Brad Shear and Secretary Helen O'Malley. Introductions were made, and the guests then chatted with the governor and secretary prior to the start of the reception. The Kentucky State trooper that accompanied Governor Shear and Secretary O'Malley was Trooper Ape Cornett. Ape was previously a deputy for Harlan County Sheriff J. Bert Sterling, and it was Kyle Potter that took Ape's position when he departed to join the Kentucky State Police. Trooper Cornett and Harry Kalos met and enjoyed greatly exchanging stories associated with their professions.

The president of the University of Kentucky arrived, as did several administrators and faculty who were Randy's friends and associates. Barbara Clark, a native of Harlan and a well known television news anchor for Lexington's CBS affiliate WKYT, channel 27, arrived and was soon in discussion with Renee Dubois about the impact on world news of the

Carmen sisters and their beautiful and enchanting golden anchor crosses. Randy had also invited his pastor, Dr. Gus Carl from Anchor Baptist Church in Lexington. Dr. Carl arrived and was warmly greeted and introduced by Randy. When everyone had arrived it was approximately 3:05 pm.

Randy stood at the lectern and said, "I want to welcome each of you to this afternoon's reception in honor of my friends from Spain and France. I think each of you has now had the pleasure to meet each of them. They are truly delightful people. Elisabeth and Henriette Carmen, Renee Dubois, and Harry Kalos have become very special to me, and I know you'll enjoy your time with them this afternoon. I wanted them to have as much time as possible to meet and talk with each of you, so we'll dispense with any more speeches. I do, however, want to point out that the Seibert, Pelle, and Helena anchor crosses are available for your inspection. Their display cases are open, and you are encouraged to pick them up for your close personal inspection. Also, Elisabeth and Henriette are wearing their beautiful anchor crosses, and I know you'll appreciate seeing those as well. Again, I would like to thank each of you for being here today, and for your interest in the amazing stories behind the Anchor Crosses. Please now continue to enjoy our guests, to view the crosses, and even to have some additional lemonade and cookies. Thank you."

Randy received a good round of applause, after which everyone continued to enjoy the reception.

And then an amazing thing happened. Trooper Ape Cornett and Harry Kalos were standing near the entrance door talking shop. Harry glanced at his watch and noticed it was just after 3:15 pm. All of a sudden the entrance door was pushed open with great force, slamming loudly into the wall at the end of its swing, and in rushed what was later to be reported by Barbara Clark on her television news program as one of the weirdest sights she had ever encountered. Two men ran into the room wearing janitors uniforms and gas masks. They were about 10 feet into the room before they realized that everyone in the room had stopped talking with each other and were now staring at them wide-eyed with mouths open in disbelief. They stopped in their tracks. The last thing either of them later remembered about the event was the sharp blow to their heads. Barbara Clark's report continued on as follows:

After the two would-be thieves broke into the room, Kentucky State Police Trooper Ape Cornett and Harry Kalos, special security agent for the Carmen Twins, each hit the back of the head of one of the intruders with the butt of their revolver, rendering them unconscious, and they collapsed onto the floor. Fortunately, Cornett and Kalos were standing beside the entrance door, and after the would-be robbers came racing into the room Cornett and Kalos were standing directly behind them. The two intruders were then taken into custody and taken to jail.

The fact that the intruders were wearing gas masks invoked an intensive search of the room for a source of gas. Two strange canisters were discovered in the room's air-conditioning ducts, and were assumed to be filled with some type of gas that could have rendered everyone in the room unconscious if exposed to it. It was further assumed that some kind of malfunction had occurred such that the canisters did not release their gas. Further tests will reveal what kind of gas was in the canisters.

One of the intruders was carrying a black trash bag, and it was assumed that the priceless golden anchor crosses were to be placed in it. Also, some kind of remote control boxes were found just outside the entrance door, and it was thought by police that these devices were made to remotely trigger the gas release from the canisters.

In talking with the Carmen Twins immediately after the incident they told me that the anchor crosses they were wearing as necklaces started to get very hot just as the intruders entered the room. They said that this strange occurrence happened anytime they were wearing the crosses and their lives became in danger. They attributed the power of the anchor crosses to preventing all those in the room from being exposed to the gas. They said the malfunction of the remote triggering device was brought about by the mysterious anchor crosses. The unknown mechanism by which this happens is always accompanied by the anchor crosses getting very warm, which was what the sisters felt. They attributed their safety and that of all those in the *room to being protected by the amazing, mysterious power of the beautiful, golden anchor crosses.*

I'm Barbara Clark for WKYT news.

The intrusion of the two robbers caused momentary panic in the reception, but as soon as the two were captured everyone seemed to recover quickly.

Randy went again to the dais and spoke into the microphone, "Friends, if I could have your attention. I apologize for the intrusion. As you can see, the police have removed the two would-be robbers, and I think the threat is gone. We have secured the three resident anchor crosses back into their cases, and the police have asked if we could move our reception to another room to allow them to carefully examine this room in an attempt to locate any sources of gas that might have been hidden here by the robbers. Fortunately, the Center has another room large enough to accommodate us. So if you would please follow me into our conference room. We have removed the normal table and chairs there, and I think there will be adequate room for us to continue visiting with each other and you will still be able to admire the two beautiful anchor crosses worn by the Carmen sisters. Please follow me."

As everyone moved from the anchor cross display room to the conference room P Rat Cook was leaving the building at the conclusion of his work shift. When he saw the crowd moving from one room to the other he realized that something must have gone wrong with the plan. He thought, 'I guess I'll have to wait a while for that new car and vacation to Europe that I had been looking forward to'. He left the building just hoping that the police wouldn't find out about his part in the failed robbery.

•••

Big Jim and Mad Mike were sitting in their jail cell. Mad Mike said, "I just don't understand what could have gone wrong. We did everything exactly as we were supposed to. That damn Mac Woolums must have messed up the gizmos that were suppose to release the gas when you pressed those remote buttons. I don't know what else it could have been."

Big Jim said, "Yeah, that's likely it. Mac must have screwed up. And now look where it's got us."

"I was never as shocked in my entire life as I was when we rushed in that door and saw all those people staring at us," Mad Mike replied. "They were all suppose to be lying flat out cold on the floor, and there they were standing up and staring at us. I'll have bad dreams about that for the rest of my life."

"Me too," said Big Jim. "and to then have the bad luck to have those two security guys be right behind us and whack us in the head. What a bummer. And now I've got a world-class headache to boot."

"Well, they say we'll go before the judge in the morning. What kind of a story are we going to tell him Big Jim?" asked Mad Mike.

"I'm not sure right now, but we've got overnight to come up with some kind of tale for him, and it better be good," answered Big Jim.

•••

Friday morning Big Jim and Mad Mike were taken to the courtroom of Judge K.S. Foster.

The bailiff announced the Judge, who then said, "Mr. Owens and Mr. Hatfield, you have been charged with breaking and entering with the intent to commit robbery. Do you have an attorney?"

Big Jim said, "No, Judge, they tried to give us one but we'd rather represent ourselves and tell you exactly what happened, if that's okay?"

Judge Foster replied, "Well, you know what they say about one who represents himself, but it's okay with me if you're sure you want to. So tell me what happened"

Big Jim started, "Well, it's like this judge. Mad Mike, Mr. Hatfield that is, and me, we was just walking around the campus there at UK. We wanted to see what it looked like. All of a sudden this guy jumps out of some bushes and points a gun at us and tells us that we have to do like he says or we're dead. He has a bag with a couple of janitors uniforms and some gas masks in it. He makes us put on those uniforms, and then marches us over to the door going into that Center place. He pushes a button on two remote control gizmos he had, and then has us rush into the Center with gas masks on. If we made it okay, I think he was then going to come in about a minute later and rob the place. But something went wrong. I guess the people in the Center were suppose to be asleep or dead or something, but they weren't, so the guy must have taken off when he saw things weren't going right. That's exactly what happened, Judge, we swear it, don't we Mr. Hatfield?"

"That's the gospel," Mad Mike answered. "That's exactly the way it happened. We didn't do nothing wrong, Your Honor."

"Mr. Harris, you're the County Attorney, what proof do you have that what Mr. Owens and Mr. Hatfield just said is not true?"

"Judge, that's the biggest crock I ever heard," said Mr. Harris. "We caught em red handed."

"You might have caught them," said Judge Foster, "but what I asked you was what proof do you have that their stories are not true?"

"Well," replied Mr. Harris, "I can't prove what they said is not true, but we certainly didn't see anyone else outside, and there's no evidence to support what they say."

Judge Foster said, "The burden of proof rests with you Mr. Harris. Did these two hurt anyone or do anything that you can charge them with and have evidence to prove the charge?"

Mr. Harris slowly nodded his head from side to side and replied, "I guess not, your honor."

"Then I have no recourse but to release them. Gentlemen, you are free to go."

Big Jim and Mad Mike got real big smiles on their faces. They nodded their heads up and down as Big Jim said, "Thank you, your honor. Thank you very much. You have a good day!"

Chapter 23

On Interstate 75

Randy and his guests had enjoyed a leisurely Friday morning, and after having a light lunch had loaded up in a minivan that Randy had reserved for the weekend from the university's motor pool. The five of them were headed South on Interstate 75 for Harlan to attend the ACFes.

Randy spoke, "I do feel really badly about the intruders that spoiled our reception yesterday afternoon. That kind of thing normally just never happens. I guess the publicity about the anchor crosses, and especially the opportunity to try and steal all five of them at once, was just too much for those guys to resist. As it turned out, of course, they weren't successful, and really the disruption was minimal."

"You should just put it out of your mind, Randy," said Henriette. "As they say, all's well that ends well, and certainly the reception ended well. Even the governor and secretary were joking and laughing about the whole thing. Since no one was injured, except the intruders, I think the excitement was interesting. But please don't you feel badly about it."

Harry then said, "Henriette's correct Randy, the reception was an overwhelming success. And it did give Ape and me a chance to practice our trade! It was like the whole thing was choreographed. When those guys came bounding into the reception, Ape and I reached together for our pistols and swung them hitting the robbers in unison. And then they dropped to the floor as one. Taking them out went just like it was planned. Then the rest of the reception went without a hitch. Everyone had a grand time.....except those two robbers!"

"Thanks for the comments," Randy replied. "I had a phone call this morning from Judge Foster's office saying that the two had been released due to lack of evidence that they intended to rob us. The robbers had concocted a story about being forced at gunpoint to do what they did by a stranger they had encountered while walking around the campus. As stupid as that sounds, the county attorney had no actual evidence to prove differently, so the judge had to release them. I understand they were from Prestonsburg, and are likely on their way back home as we speak."

"Yeah, that story stinks," said Harry. "But I do understand."

• • •

Big Jim and Mad Mike were almost back to Prestonsburg. They had stopped at a McDonalds on the way to have lunch.

"Big Jim, when we get home are you going to get ole Mac Woolums over to tell us what he thinks went wrong?" asked Mad Mike.

"Yeah, I plan on doing that," replied Big Jim. "He probably won't admit that anything he did was to blame, but at least it'd make me feel better. I may wait till tomorrow. I need to rest up after we get home. My head's still killing me. I'm anxious to contact P Rat to see if they pinned anything on him. I hope not, so we might be able to use him again."

"You're not thinking of trying another hit there are you?" asked Mad Mike.

"I'm not thinking of anything right now. But it's always good to have options, Mad Mike. It's always good to have options."

• • •

Randy said, "I also had a call from my office this morning saying that the armored car escorted by four state police cruisers came to the Center around 10 am this morning to pick up the Seibert, Pelle, and Helena anchor crosses for transport to Harlan for the festival. So they should be there and safely positioned in the Seibert Anchor Cross Memorial by the time we arrive later today."

"Randy," Elisabeth said. "I see we're approaching a rest

area. Would you mind terribly to stop. I think I had too much tea for lunch."

"Me too," replied Renee, and Henriette nodded her head in agreement.

"Happy to stop, I need a little stretch anyway," responded Randy.

The minivan pulled into the rest area. All five headed for the restrooms. Randy and Harry came out before any of the ladies. Randy told Harry he was going to stroll around a little to stretch his legs. Harry walked to where their minivan was parked and took a seat on a bench beside the sidewalk, waiting on the ladies. Harry kept an eye looking toward the restrooms, ready to respond if he saw any sign of trouble.

A moment later Harry noticed an old car pull into a parking space between where he was seated and the restrooms. The windows in the car were down, and smoke and loud rap music was blasting out. There appeared to be three persons in the car. They just sat there. No one opened a door. They seemed to be looking toward the restrooms.

Renee then appeared leaving the restroom and walked briskly toward Harry and the minivan. When she got to Harry she told him that she too was going to walk a little further down to stretch her legs before the sisters got back, and off she trotted.

After a couple of minutes Harry saw the sisters come out of the restroom and start walking slowly toward him. At the same time the three men in the old car opened their car doors and walked onto the sidewalk and started walking slowly toward the rest rooms and the approaching sisters.

Harry didn't like what he saw. All three of the men looked like punks. All three wore jeans and t-shirts. Tattoos were plastered all over any visible skin. One had a long sliver chain hanging from a pocket. Their pants were worn so low that their underwear was clearly visible. Harry got the feeling their pants could fall down to their feet at any moment. One had spiked hair that rose about 8 inches on the top of his head. His hair was dyed a bright orange. The other two had shaved heads. They all had body piercing jewelry all over. Harry had the distinct feeling that trouble loomed ahead.

The Carmen sisters were each wearing very lovely dresses and jackets, and certainly had the conservative appearance of ladies of means. As the punks approached the sisters, Harry noticed the two on each side reach into their pockets and withdraw switchblade knives. Harry started moving fast.

The punk with the spiked hair, walking in the middle of the three, said when they had reached the sisters, "Ladies, we'll just relieve you of those purses. You hand them over real nice and we won't have to cut you up." The other two punks bringing up their switchblades and pressing the buttons to release wicked looking 6" long blades.

All three punks then got very strange looks on their faces when the reaction by the sisters was just to offer a huge smile. And they offered not their purses.

Suddenly, as the two with the knives started simultaneously to bring the blades closer toward the sisters, all three punks felt something hit hard behind their knees, causing all three to fall over backwards. When they fell they landed on Harry, who had run up behind them and at the last moment thrown himself horizontal into the legs of the three punks. Then with one mighty grab Harry got each of his hands outside the heads of the two punks with the switchblades such that he then had all three of their heads between his hands. And with one mighty effort he then tried to bring his hands together, slamming the three heads with a force that caused them to immediately black out and fall helplessly to the ground.

Harry then stood and walked around in front of the three and stooped to gather their knives. He then looked at the still smiling sisters and said, "Ladies, I hope these gentlemen didn't cause you a problem."

"No problem at all, Harry," Elisabeth said "We saw you coming to our rescue and knew we didn't have to worry. As always, you protected us real well"

"Yes, thank you Harry," said Henriette.

Just then a uniformed security guard from the rest area came running to the scene. Harry and the sisters explained what had happened, and Harry gave the guard the two switchblades. He rolled the three punks over, placed handcuffs on them, and then used his hand-held radio to call the Kentucky State Police. He was taking a written statement when Randy and Renee got back from their walks. They were astounded to see three handcuffed men sitting on the ground, a uniformed officer writing up a report, and a smiling and pleasant Elisabeth, Henriette, and Harry.

"I can't wait to hear the story behind this," Renee said.

"Wasn't much, really," replied Harry. "I'll tell you all about it when we resume our trip to Harlan."

The Kentucky State Police arrived and after talking with the guard took a copy of his report and then placed the three men in his cruiser. He called for a wrecker to pick up their car. He then walked over to the minivan where all five were standing, and said, "I would like to thank you for what you did. Those three hoodlums have been robbing people all up and down interstate 75 for several months. They are from Chicago. Until now they had been successful in targeting people that they thought would have money and not resist them. I guess they met their match in Mr. Harry Kalos here. With your statement and the statements of previous victims I feel certain we can put them away for a good long time. Thanks again. You folks drive carefully."

Harry replied, "Thanks officer, glad to be of assistance."

All five got back in the minivan, and were again on their way to Harlan.

Harry told the story in detail to Randy and Renee. Renee had her notebook out and was frantically taking notes. This incident would provide the basis for a very interesting story in **Le Monde.**

After Harry finished his version of what had happened, Henriette said, "Elisabeth and I were not the least bit concerned. It helped a lot that we could clearly see Harry behind those hoodlums, but also we knew we were in no danger at all because we each felt heat coming from our anchor crosses that we're wearing. So if Harry had not been able to save us, we know the power of the anchor crosses would have. That's why we both had big smiles."

The minivan continued toward Harlan.

Chapter 24

Harlan, Kentucky

Everything seemed to be going well. Fred could even faintly hear the rock band playing across the street at the initial ACFes activities on the stage in front of the court house. Fred had just gotten back to Creech Cafe after making some introductory remarks at 2 pm, opening the festival activities. The crowd wasn't real large yet, but a couple of hundred had gathered for the opening event, and everyone seemed to be enjoying listening to the music. Fred had elected to come back to his business. He could still see the court house out the front windows of his business......so if anything needed his attention he could be back across the street quickly. One thing bothered him a bit. There was a big blue van parked almost in front of his store. Fortunately, it was parked far enough East that he could still see the court house. It had been parked there now for a couple of days, but

Fred figured it belonged to one of the contractors working on the ACFes, so he didn't think much more about it.

The armored truck with the 4 state police car escort had arrived in Harlan just before the opening ceremony. The three anchor crosses had been placed in the Seibert Anchor Cross Memorial on the Northwest corner of the court house property, and the state police troopers had remained at the Memorial as security for the valuable golden artifacts. The Memorial had been opened to the public following the opening ceremony on the court house stage. Lots of people had been filing through the Memorial, and there was now a line with about 10 people standing outside waiting to get in. Fred knew that most all these people represented folks from outside Harlan who had never had the chance to see the anchor crosses before. That put a smile on his face. New visitors meant new money to the city. That's exactly what Fred had hoped for with ACFes. He just hoped that everything would continue to go smoothly.

●●●

Knoxville, Tennessee

The junkyard gang was arguing again.

"Hell no, I ain't going out there and practice the heist again," screamed Eagle Eye. "We've practiced the thing till I'm sick of it already."

Bad Eye replied, "I just don't see what's wrong with

practicing. We've only gone over it about 4 times since Jones got back and gave us the information about where the display cases are located that have the expensive stuff in them. We need to make sure everyone knows exactly where they are so we don't waste time looking. That's what the practice is all about."

"We all know where the good stuff is located," said Eagle Eye. "Once you know, what good does it do to keep going over it? I feel certain all of us knows exactly what we are to do and when we're to do it. That ain't what I'm worried about."

"What you worried about, Eagle Eye?" asked Snake.

"I'm still thinking we're just asking for it with the Kentucky State Police post 10 located right across the road from the mall. It wouldn't take them a minute to be at the DiamondCraft if they got a call," said Eagle Eye.

"You worry too much," said Bad Eye. "I've told you that every officer they have will be downtown on duty at the festival. That post 10 will be deserted. The only person in the whole building will be the dispatcher, and he sure as hell can't leave to come over to the mall. You're just all upset over nothing. Put it out of your mind. It's not a problem."

Billie, Jones, and Snake all nodded their heads in agreement as Eagle Eye replied, "I just hope you're right. If they had even one trooper hanging out at post 10 and they got a call reporting us robbing the DiamondCraft our goose would be cooked."

Snake then said, "Like Bad Eye said, Eagle Eye, just put it out of your mind. Everything will go smooth as a ribbon."

"I hope so, Snake, I sure hope so," replied Eagle Eye.

●●●

Harlan, Kentucky

Sheriff J. Bert Sterling and Deputy Kyle Potter walked into Creech Drug.

"Howdy Lawmen, Howdy Lawmen," Polly squawked.

"Afternoon bird," Bert replied, as he reached up and stroked the parrot, and then he and Kyle walked to a table and sat.

Fred came bounding over with coffee, and then sat to join them. He said, "Everything seem to be going well with the festival as far as you know?"

Kyle replied, "So far, so good. The music sounds great, and there's a big line now waiting to get inside the Memorial to see the three anchor crosses. Security looks good everywhere. Folks are buying goodies from all the street vendors. Yeah, I think all is under control Mr. Mayor."

Bert then said, "Tomorrow will be the real challenge, Fred. But I got a feeling everything's going to go well then too. You've done a superb job of planning this whole thing, and Harlan will certainly benefit. Have you heard any word from Randy and his guests?"

Fred replied, "Randy called me on his cell just a few minutes ago. They're on their way. He said something about having a little trouble at a rest stop, but that everything was fine and that they should arrive here in Harlan around 4 o'clock."

"I'm anxious to get the full story on what happened at the reception yesterday afternoon. It sounded like it could have been very serious, but fortunately turned out okay," said Kyle.

"Yeah," Fred replied. "We'll learn more about it after they get here."

As they finished their coffee Bert said, "We just wanted to drop in to make sure you were satisfied with everything, Fred. And of course the coffee was great as always. We better head back over to the office."

"Just real quick, before you go," Fred said, "I just posted a new article up on the wall over there," as he pointed to the far wall. "Got just a second to hear the story.....it'll make you leave with a smile!"

"Go," Bert and Kyle said in unison.

Fred continued, "It goes something like this. A teacher noticed that a little boy sitting at the back of her class was squirming around, scratching his crotch, and not paying attention. She went back to find out what was going on with him, and found he was very embarrassed as he whispered to her that he had just recently been circumcised and he was quite itchy. The teacher then told him to go to the principal's office to call his mother and ask her what he should do about it. He did, and then returned to class. Suddenly there was a big commotion at the back of the room and the teacher went to investigate. She found the boy sitting at his desk with his 'private part' hanging out. The teacher then said, "I thought

I told you to call your mom!" The boy replied, "I did. She told me if I could stick it out till noon she'd come and pick me up!"

Bert and Kyle left Creech Cafe with big grins on their faces.

Chapter 25

Harlan, Kentucky

etty Bell had once again proven what a superb cook she was. Pastor Raymond and Betty had invited all the members of the ACFes committee to join with Randy and his guests for dinner at their home on Friday evening. After a wonderful meal they retired to the living room.

Patting his stomach, Randy said, "I know I speak for everyone when I extend my deepest thanks to Betty for that outstanding meal." Everyone nodded in agreement, and then applause broke out with everyone looking and smiling toward Betty.

When the applause died down, Betty replied, "Thank you. But you know how much I enjoy cooking, and it's just a big honor to have each of you here in our home and to be able to have you for a meal."

Raymond then said, "I think the only new visitor we have

this evening is Harry Kalos. I enjoyed talking with Harry over our meal, and we're honored to have him as our guest. I know that he, Bert, and Kyle have a lot of professional things to talk about, but I did want to thank Harry again for his very able assistance in preventing those two attempted robberies, the one at the reception yesterday afternoon, and the other earlier today at the rest area. Certainly things could have been vastly different had either of those been successful, and very likely several people could have been seriously hurt. So a big thanks to Harry, and a big welcome to Harlan." Another round of applause was given in honor of Harry.

Harry blushed, and said, "Thank you my friends. What I did was just my duty, nothing more. It is wonderful to have the opportunity to visit here, and I thank you so much for your hospitality."

Raymond continued, "Thanks Harry. And I would be remiss if I didn't say once again what an honor it is to have the Carmen sisters as guests here in our home. It's not real often that royalty makes it to Harlan, but it did once again today. We're so grateful to Elisabeth and Henriette for taking the time and making the effort to come here and to share their astounding anchor crosses. And let me also take the opportunity to thank Renee Dubois for her critical part in ACFes. The Carmen sisters wouldn't be here if it were not for Renee's knowledge about the anchor crosses and her contacting Randy. We all hope you have a wonderful visit here in Harlan and that you tremendously enjoy the festival."

Mayor Fred Knapp said, "Here, here. Well spoken Raymond. As mayor I can assure you that you are our honored guests, and you do indeed have the key to our fair city. We just can't thank you enough for the effort you made to be here. I am pleased to report that all the festival activities today went extremely well. The opening ceremony was attended by a couple hundred people, but many more arrived here during the day. Our town is packed with visitors, and it seems a good time is being had by all. And, I might add, it certainly pleases the mayor to no end!"

Kyle then said, "And we're all looking forward to tomorrow. I just hope we can accommodate all those that come to ACFes. One thing that I really regret is not having pictures of those would-be robbers that Harry took care of. I'd sure have enjoyed seeing the looks on their faces when they encountered Harry."

Randy replied, "I think your wish has been granted, Kyle. I knew that Barbara Clark used her cell phone to snap a picture of the two robbers wearing their gas masks just after they broke into the reception yesterday, and I asked her to send me a copy, which she did. And then I did use my cell to snap a picture of the three punks laying on the ground out cold after Harry's flying tackle and head crushing. I plan to have hard copies made of them, and I'll see that you all get copies, but for now I'll just pass my cell phone around and you can look at them."

Big laughs and smiles came from each person as Randy's phone was passed around and everyone saw the pictures.

The group continued to enjoy each other's company for about another hour, and then adjourned for the evening.

Tomorrow was the big day!

Chapter 26

Harlan, Kentucky

It was Saturday morning. Governor Shear and Secretary O'Malley arrived at the court house at 9:30 am. Mayor Knapp had been awaiting their arrival, knowing that State Police trooper Ape Cornett, who would be driving them, would park in a reserved space behind the court house. Fred had introduced a favorite music group that started performing on the court house stage at 9 am. He had then left the stage and walked around behind the court house to greet the Governor and Secretary when they arrived, and had then escorted them to their convertible car that would be second in the parade through downtown Harlan starting at 10 am. Mayor Knapp would also ride in the second car with the Governor and Secretary. The parade was forming down Central Street, with the lead car being at the corner of Third and Central streets with the rest of the parade forming behind it, winding back to the Harlan Elementary School, then up the hill to Mound Street, and continuing west on Mound Street for several blocks. The Carmen Twins, as the honored guests, would sit in the lead car. Since they were wearing their beautiful golden anchor crosses extra security had been assigned to their car. Harry Kalos and three Kentucky State Troopers would be walking beside their car, two on each side.

Governor Shear knew that Trooper Ape Cornett was originally from Harlan, and after Ape had delivered the Governor and Secretary to Mayor Knapp, the Governor suggested that Ape might wish to visit some friends in Harlan during the morning, since adequate security had already been established for the parade and the following stage sessions this morning. Sheriff Sterling and Deputy Potter had accompanied Mayor Knapp to meet the Governor and Secretary. Since Kyle and Ape were also good friends, Kyle having taken Ape's position when Ape resigned from the Sheriff's department to pursue a career at the Kentucky State Police, Ape asked Kyle if he would like to accompany him up to Post 10 to visit with their good friend Clayton Squibb. Clayton had been a Kentucky State Trooper for almost 30 years at Harlan's Post 10, but after encountering some physical problems had been assigned the job of dispatcher there. Kyle jumped at the chance to visit with them, so the two left in Ape's unmarked State Police Cruiser to drive up to visit Clayton at Post 10 while the parade and morning ceremonies on the court house stage were going on.

•••

"I'm thirsty.....it's hot as hell in this car," said Snake Potter.

"Shut up, Snake," Bad Eye replied. "We've just got to sit here until we're sure the parade is underway downtown, and then we make our hit. Once that parade is underway traffic will be backed up so bad that it will be impossible for anyone to get out of there, including the cops. That's important for us. It's almost 10 am now, so we'll just sit here another 10 minutes or so. You can make it that long."

Bad Eye, Snake, Eagle Eye, Jones, and Billie were all crammed in Bad Eye's 15 year old Chevy Impala. Bad Eye and Snake were in the front seats. The other three were in the back. They were parked in the center of the Village Mall parking lot, waiting for the appointed time to move their car to the curb just outside the entrance doors that lead to the DiamondCraft jewelry store.

•••

Clayton Squibb looked up from his dispatcher station at the Kentucky State Police Post 10 headquarters and said, "I don't believe my eyes!! It looks just like my two good buddies Kyle Potter and Ape Cornett!! Is it an apparition, or is it actually you?"

Trooper Cornett replied, "Your eyes do not deceive you, Clayton. Kyle and I were granted a little break from all the festivities downtown, and we elected to come visit a few minutes with you. It's not often we get to see you anymore, and even though you're on duty, and we certainly don't want to distract you, we thought we might scrounge a cup of coffee and sit here and talk when you weren't busy."

Clayton walked from behind his desk and gave both Kyle and Ape a hand shake and big hug, and said, "Guys, it's just really good to see you both. You look great. The coffee's right there behind you. Grab a cup, and then we'll talk and get caught up a bit. Things are actually pretty slow right now. All the activity in the county is pretty much downtown for the festival. All our troopers are down there, so I think we should be good to talk uninterrupted."

Kyle and Ape nodded in agreement and turned to get their coffee. Clayton returned to his desk. The two visitors then pulled up chairs in front of Claytons desk and the three friends began talking.

●●●

"Okay, guys, I think we should be good to go," Bad Eye said. "The parade should be underway downtown. Just remember exactly how we planned everything. Don't screw this up."

Bad Eye started the car, and drove slowly across the Village Mall parking lot toward the entrance to the mall that lead to DiamondCraft. He pulled the car directly in front of the entrance door and stopped. He left the engine running and turned on the cars's emergency lights. Snake, sitting in the front passenger seat beside Bad Eye, opened his door and got out of the car. Eagle Eye, Jones, and Billie emerged from the crowded back seat and joined Snake just outside the entrance door. All the windows were down in the car, and Snake turned back just as the four were about to enter the Mall and shouted at Bad Eye, "You keep that damn engine running.....we want a quick get-away when we come out!"

"Just do your part, Snake, I'll do mine," Bad Eye shouted back.

Each of the four would-be robbers carried a cloth bag large enough to hold the jewelry they planned to steal. In each bag was a cloth head mask that fitted over their entire head with cut outs for their eyes and nose. They would pull these out and put them on just before reaching the jewelry store. Also in each cloth bag was a pistol.

• • •

Inside DiamondCraft three employees were working. There were no customers currently in the store. Penny, Andrew, and Mike were located at different areas in the shop. Penny was restocking some display counters, Andrew was making repairs, and Mike, the owner, was sitting at his desk doing paperwork.

Suddenly the three heard a loud voice say, "Everyone stand up and put your hands up over your head, NOW...... DO IT."

Penny, already standing, stared at the four hooded robbers holding guns, and immediately shot her hands up into the air. Andrew and Mike stood immediately and raised their hands above their heads. Mike yelled at the robbers, "No problem....please, I don't want anyone hurt. We'll do whatever you say."

As Mike spoke, he slowly moved his right foot to a button on the floor beside his desk. The button, when pressed, sent a silent signal to the Kentucky State Police Post 10 that indicated a robbery was in progress. There had been several poorly attempted robberies at DiamonCraft in the past, and Mike had installed the system just about a year ago. This was the first time he had used it. He said a silent prayer that it would work, and pressed the button.

Snake said, "I want each of you to move right over here to this wall with your hands up. You do as you're told and you'll not be shot. You make one false move and you're dead."

The three slowly moved to the wall with their hands remaining above their heads, and they stood there.

Snake then said, "We'll all be keeping an eye on you..... one move and it's all over."

All four then went quickly to their preassigned display cases, opened them, and began to gather the jewelry in their cloth bags. All glanced at the three employees frequently, and had stuck their guns in their belts. The three employees remained motionless, and the robbery proceeded as planned.

●●●

Back at Kentucky State Police Post 10 headquarters Clayton was saying, "Yeah, if I can make it another couple of years I plan to retire. I look forward to taking off in my motor home and finding a lot of good fishing spots. Although my health has been going South, I can still get around okay. I just hope the good Lord will grant me sufficient health and time to enjoy my retirement."

"I predict that will happen," Kyle replied. "Maybe Ape and I can arrange to meet you somewhere after your retire and help you catch a few of those big ones!"

Ape then said, "I hear a beeping noise.....what's that all about?"

Clayton looked immediately up at his display screen and saw the red flashing light that identified a robbery in progress at DiamondCraft. He said, "We got trouble. Apparently there's a robbery taking place at DiamondCraft, and I know all our troopers are tied up downtown in the parade. There's no way they could get up here in time."

Kyle jumped up from his seat and said, "No problem Clayton, Ape and I are on our way. It's just across the street, we can be there in a couple of minutes. We'll take care of it."

Clayton responded, "Hey guys, I hate to break up our nice conversation, and I sure hate to send you into harm's way, but it looks like that's the only option I have. Please hurry, and do be very careful. Give me a call back when you get a chance."

"Will do," Ape replied, as the two of them rushed out the door and into Ape's unmarked state police cruiser. They left Post 10 in a hurry, but without their lights or siren turned on.

• • •

Bad Eye sat in his car with the motor running. He looked at his watch. It had been about 5 minutes since the four had entered the mall. He knew they should be finishing up the robbery and coming out momentarily. He kept looking all around the parking lot, but had only seen a few cars park and shoppers get out and walk into other mall entrances. No one had gone in the entrance where his car was parked. He then noticed a large, black sedan pull into the parking lot and park off to his left and behind him. At that moment he was distracted by a couple that had walked in front of his car and headed into the mall leading to DiamondCraft. He carefully followed the couple's movement.

After Ape had parked his unmarked cruiser, and when Bad Eye's attention was turned to the couple walking in front of his car, Kyle jumped out of the cruiser and ran to the back of Bad Eye's car and stooped down out of sight. He then moved leaned over and with bent knees up to the side of the car to the driver's door. Just as Bad Eye turned his head back from watching the couple enter the mall he felt cold steel touch his left temple.

"Don't even think about drawing your gun, Bad Eye," Kyle said. "In case you're wondering, that's my gun you feel pressing on your temple. Step out of the car, and keep both of your hands up." Kyle pulled the driver's side door open. Bad Eye emerged.

"Take off your eye patch, and do it now," Kyle said. "And give me your baseball hat."

Kyle had removed his dress jacket and his tie in Ape's cruiser, and had his blue shirt collar unbuttoned. Fortunately, Bad Eye was also wearing a blue shirt, and the two were about the same size.

Ape came running up, grabbed Bad Eye and took him to his cruiser, placed him in the back seat, handcuffed him to a metal bar and then got in the driver's seat of his car.

Kyle put Bad Eye's eye patch and baseball hat on and jumped into Bad Eye's car. He looked over toward the mall entrance and did not see anyone. He sat in the car with the motor still running.

About a minute later the entrance door to the mall flew open and the four with hoods removed and carrying their cloth bags came running out and jumped into the car. Three crowded into the rear seat, and one jumped into the passenger seat beside Kyle.

"Okay Bad Eye, hit it. We got all the good stuff, let's get out of here," Snake said.

But the car didn't move.

At the same time that Snake looked directly at Kyle and

realized he wasn't Bad Eye, a revolver was stuck through the driver's side open rear window and Ape said to all in the back seat, "You three just slowly raise your hands above your head. Kyle, you got your dad covered?"

Kyle raised his right hand and pointed his revolver directly in the face of his father Snake, and said, "Hi Dad. Fancy meeting your here......please raise your hands."

The color drained from Snake's face as he raised his hands. He said, "We weren't suppose to meet like this. How the hell did you get here?"

Kyle responded, "Not important. Just keep your hands up or I'll become fatherless, and believe me when I say I would do it."

"Everyone out of the car with your hands up," Ape said as he opened the rear driver's side door.

Kyle, keeping his gun aimed squarely at Snake, opened the driver's door and got out, motioning for Snake to follow him. Snake complied.

Handcuffs were then placed on all five of the crooks. Their guns and cloth bags were confiscated, and Eagle Eye and Jones were taken by Ape back to his cruiser and placed in the back seat along with Bad Eye. Billie and Snake were placed in the back seat of Bad Eye's car. The two cars then left the Mall and traveled across the street to the Kentucky State Police Post 10 headquarters.

"Hey Clayton, got five customers for you," Ape shouted as the five were paraded into the Headquarters' office.

"My, my," Clayton said. "What in the world do we have here?"

Kyle replied, "Well, we got my father and four other scum-bags. I think it's Bad Eye Cawood's old junk yard gang plus a bonus.....Eagle Eye Looney. They tried to rob the DiamondCraft. Think you can hold them till Monday? I'm sure Judge Oakes will be able to see them then."

"No problem," Clayton replied. "I've got five real comfortable jail cells here where we can accommodate them till their appearance on Monday."

The five were then marched to the holding cells and locked up.

Back in the headquarters' office Clayton said, "Guys, I can't believe we were that lucky. If you two had not been here, they would undoubtedly have gotten away with the robbery. I'll make sure that the **Harlan Daily Enterprise** gets all the details about what happened, and I'm sure your excellent performance today will get entered into your service records. You certainly acted quickly and decisively. And had you not come up with the plan for Kyle to dress like Bad Eye and fool the other four into getting trapped in the car, I feel certain there would have been shooting and very likely someone would have gotten either hurt or killed. I certainly thank you."

The three friends shook hands and exchanged hugs. Ape and Kyle got back in Ape's cruiser. Before they started to drive Ape said, "Well Kyle, that little visit certainly proved most interesting. I really feel good about being able to capture those crooks, and to prevent the robbery, but I felt very badly that you encountered your father under such bad circumstances. I know it must have been hard to catch him in an attempted robbery, and then to have to bring him in at gunpoint."

Kyle replied, "Thanks for the kind words, Ape, but my father has been nothing but trouble for my mother and me. I understand from mother that at one point in time he was a gentle, caring, and lovable man. But that was only when he was sober, and his drinking continuously got worse. He wound up being a major problem for mom. When he was drunk, which was most of the time, he would beat her and just make her life miserable. And he was never kind to me. Things came to a breaking point when he was involved in that attempted bank robbery. If things had gone as they had planned he would have killed both mom and me, sealing us up in the bank vault along with several other people. But the good Lord was looking after us, and through the mysterious power of the Seibert Anchor Cross we were spared from death. Shortly after that episode mother got a divorce and dad went to jail. Neither of us had seen him again until today. And while it is certainly sad to see him under these circumstances, I just feel pity and am sorry for him. He made the choice to take the low road, just as did the other four. I'm just glad we caught them and prevented them from possibly doing harm to others. Hope springs eternal, so perhaps one fine day out there somewhere in the future they will see and understand the error of their ways and turn their lives around, and maybe even give their lives to the Lord. But for the present, I just feel good that they are going to jail."

"I understand," said Ape. "If it's okay with you, I'd like to make a stop at DiamondCraft to return their jewelry."

"Great. I'm sure they will welcome us with open arms!" Kyle replied.

Ape drove back across highway 421 into the Village Mall and parked close to the entrance to DiamondCraft. The two got out with the bags full of jewelry and headed into the mall.

Mike saw them coming, and said, "Welcome, welcome, welcome, my friends! You just don't know how much we appreciate what you did. Not only did you recover the stolen jewelry, but you prevented anyone from getting hurt. I just find it hard to find the proper words to convey my true feelings."

"Not necessary," replied Ape. "We just did our duty. But certainly we were very fortunate to be at Post 10 when they attempted the robbery. The timing could not have been better. Your silent alarm system worked like a charm!"

After giving back the stolen jewelry and saying goodbye to Mike, Andrew, and Penny, Ape and Kyle returned to Ape's cruiser and headed to Pastor Bell's home for lunch.

Chapter 27

Harlan, Kentucky

In fact, the home of Pastor and Betty Bell was located in Browning Acres, only a few blocks from the Village Mall, and took Ape and Kyle only a couple of minutes to get there. The Bells had invited the governor, the economic development secretary, Mayor Knapp, the Carmen Twins, Renee Dubois, Harry Kalos, Dr. Peters, Sheriff Sterling, Trooper Ape Cornett, and Deputy Kyle Potter and his mother Carolyn. Because of the large number of people and the time constraint to get lunch and back to the court house in plenty of time for the start of the 1 pm ceremony Betty had prepared a simple buffet lunch consisting of soup, sandwiches, potato salad, cookies, coffee and sweet tea. The luncheon was to start at 11:30 am, and conclude no later than 12:15 in order to allow time to drive back into town and get everything all set up for the afternoon program.

Everyone other than Ape and Kyle had already arrived at the Bell's home. The parade downtown took place from 10 to 11 am, and then several politicians spoke at the court house until noon. The entourage going to lunch at the Bells left from the court house at about 11:15 am, bypassing some of the political speeches.   At exactly 11:30 Pastor Bell welcomed everyone for lunch, said a prayer, and the group started filling their plates from the buffet set up in Betty's kitchen and then took a seat at the large dining room table. There was seating for 14. After everyone had found a seat and started to eat, Trooper Cornett and Deputy Potter arrived at the Bell's home, filled their plates, and then took the last two chairs at about 11:45 am. They explained why they were late, and kept the group entertained during lunch by telling about their visit with Clayton Squibb at Post 10 and the subsequent arrest of the thieves at the DiamondCraft jewelry store.

After hearing the story Sheriff Sterling said, "That's the best news I've heard in quite a while! Not only did you very expertly stop the robbery without anyone getting hurt, but you arrested five real hoodlums. I had been wondering what happened to Bad Eye Cawood's junk yard gang after they got out of prison, and Eagle Eye Looney had disappeared about a year ago after he failed to take me out on three different occasions. Then he showed up again at Maggard's grocery a few weeks ago trying to fence some stolen diamonds, but he managed to escape. I guess we now know he joined up with the junk yard gang. That all five of them are now in jail is like an early Christmas gift for me. Governor Shear, we certainly made a good decision to send Ape and Kyle up to visit Clayton Squibb this morning!"

Governor Shear replied, "Indeed we did. What a fantistic job you two guys accomplished. I know Bert will properly reward Deputy Potter for his excellent work, and I'll make sure that Trooper Cornett's part is on record with the State Police. You two are a great credit to your profession."

Ape and Kyle beamed, and nodded their heads approvingly toward the governor.

Secretary O'Malley then said, "And before we get back to the festival, I think we need to express our appreciation to Pastor and Betty Bell for hosting this excellent, efficient luncheon for us."

A big round of applause was given the Bells, and then everyone began to exit.

* * *

At exactly noon Badass Brown heard three knocks on the back door of his van. He felt great relief. He had been so afraid that ole Bennie would be drunk and let him down. Plan A still was on!

He opened the door, and there stood Bennie with a big smile on his face. He said, "See, I told you I could do it. It's noon and I'm here just like you told me to be!"

"Come in, come in, quick, before someone sees you," Badass replied as Bennie entered the van and Badass shut the door behind him.

Badass said, "Okay, here's the drone and the cell phone. Remember, you call me just as soon as you see the sheriff's car approaching his parking space. And make sure the drone is sitting on the ground and good to go. Stay clear of the drone, and then just watch it until you see the grenade start to drop. Then duck back behind the wall and wait for the explosion. I'll see you at your house after you get the two golden things off those Carmen sisters. Then we'll be on easy street!"

"You make it sound easy, Badass," Bennie replied. "I just hope it goes as planned."

"It will," Badass replied. "Now get out of here and get everything all ready to go behind the court house. You watch real good for the sheriff."

Badass opened the van's back door and Bennie left with the bag containing the drone and cell phone.

•••

The Bells did an excellent job of keeping their luncheon exactly on time. Everyone had departed by about 12:20 pm. Bert told Kyle that he wanted him and Ape to accompany Randy Peters to the Seibert Memorial to remove the Seibert, Pelle, and Helena Anchor Crosses and bring them to the court house stage for the afternoon ceremony. The idea was that all five of the crosses would be displayed. The Carmen Sisters would each wear their anchor cross, Kyle would wear the Seibert anchor cross, Bert would wear the Pelle anchor cross, and Pastor Raymond Bell would wear the Helena anchor cross. All would be on the stage.

Bert gathered the Carmen Sisters, Renee Dubois, and Harry Kalos to ride in his car back to town. They departed for the court house.

•••

Bennie was all set. He had the drone positioned on the ground about 10 feet away from him, and he stood with cell phone in hand peeking around the corner at the back of the court house. He had used extra will-power to refrain from excess drinking this morning, but his hands were beginning to shake. He would sure be relieved to have all this over.

He then saw the sheriff's car approaching his parking space. He jerked up the cell phone and punched in Badass's number. Badass answered on the first ring.

Bennie said, "Hey Badass, the sheriff's car is right now pulling into his parking space. Better get the drone up and going."

Bennie immediately heard and saw the propellers start to turn on the drone. Then it began its assent. Bennie was amazed at how well Badass could control it. He figured he must have gotten in a lot of practice. It rose higher and higher. Then it started to move over above Bert's car. It looked as though it was perfectly positioned above the car maybe 500 feet or so up in the air. The moment had arrived. Bennie strained to see if the gizmo that released the grenade was operating. It looked as though he could see some movement on the drone, but he didn't see the door-thing open to drop the grenade.

The movement that Bennie saw on the drone was the actuator that pulled the pin from the grenade. Once the pin was pulled and the safety lever released, the grenade would explode in 5 seconds. After pulling the pin the slider was suppose to open to allow the grenade to drop from the drone and release the safety lever. Only it didn't! The movement caused by the mechanism pulling the pin caused the grenade to roll releasing the safety lever, but the slider that the grenade rested on failed to open. The active grenade was trapped on the drone.

One thousand one, one thousand two, one thousand three, one thousand four, one thousand five.............BOOM!

Bennie had not ducked back behind the corner of the court house building because he had not seen the grenade start to drop. He was still watching the drone. What he saw was the drone exploding with a tremendous noise, and pieces from the grenade and drone flying in every direction.

The crowd in the front of the court house awaiting the start of the afternoon program all looked up in the sky toward the explosion. They then broke into a loud applause, thinking that the explosion was some kind of fireworks associated with the festival to mark the beginning of the afternoon session.

Directly below the explosion none of the five in the sheriff's car had gotten out. They started to feel some of the debris from the explosion start to hit the top of the car. Harry said, "I don't know what that explosion was, but everyone just sit tight for a moment." The two men were in the front seat, with the three ladies seated in the rear.

Bert looked at Harry and said, "Yeah, I don't know either, but I don't like it. Whatever it was, it wasn't part of the festival."

Elisabeth said, "I certainly don't know what it was either, but I do know that our lives were in danger. My anchor cross is extremely warm, and that can only mean that something bad was about to happen and that we were saved by its miraculous power. Sister, did you feel it too?"

Henriette nodded in agreement and said, "Oh my, yes. My anchor cross feels very warm."

Renee was writing frantically in her notebook. She thought, 'This is going to be another great story!'

After another few seconds the falling debris abated. Bert and Harry opened their doors and stepped outside. Other than seeing a lot of small pieces of stuff on their car and on the ground around them, everything seemed fine. They then opened the back doors for the ladies, and the two men escorted them to the front of the court house and up on the stage.

At the sight of the explosion Bennie started to run. As soon as he got about a block away from the court house he slowed to a fast walk. He was headed home. He thought, 'I knew that damn contraption wouldn't work. That's the last time I'm going to do anything with Badass. I'll just head to the house, get a good snort, take a nap and try and forget this whole thing'.

●●●

Badass couldn't believe it. As he sat in the driver's seat of the van he had a perfect view of the explosion. He knew what had happened. The slider had failed to operate to allow the grenade to drop, and the thing exploded aboard the drone. Damn, damn, damn! All that planning and money. Plan A was a bust. He'd just have to go to Plan B.

●●●

All of the participants in the afternoon program were on the stage and seated with the exception of Randy and Kyle. All those already seated were chatting among themselves, and it was still about 5 minutes prior the scheduled start of the program. Randy, Kyle, and Ape then appeared. They had been to the Seibert Memorial to bring the other anchor crosses to the ceremony. Kyle was already wearing the Seibert anchor cross. Randy, escorted by Ape, was carrying the Pelle and Helena anchor crosses, and he walked over to Bert and placed the Pelle around his neck, and then to Pastor Bell and placed the Helena on him. Ape walked to one end of the stage and stood guard. Harry Kalos took a similar position at the other end of the stage. The program was all set to begin.

At exactly 1 pm Mayor Knapp walked to the podium and said, "My friends, it is so very good to see all of you here today. My name is Fred Knapp, and I'm proud to serve as mayor of Harlan. I'm also very proud to announce that we have the largest attendance today in the city's history for this, the first, Anchor Cross Festival. Many people worked very hard to make ACFes a success. I would like to introduce some of those at this time. You'll be hearing from many of them shortly, but for the time being please allow me to introduce those on the stage. And please hold your applause until all have been introduced. Starting on your far left, standing guard, we have State Police Trooper and former Harlan County deputy sheriff Ape Cornett, then seated we have Carolyn Potter and her son Deputy Kyle Potter, then Sheriff J. Bert Sterling, Jake Keller, Kentucky Governor Brad Shear, Elisabeth Carmen, Henriette Carmen, Kentucky Economic Development Secretary Helen O'Malley, Dr. Randy Peters, Pastor Raymond Bell, and standing guard on your right is Mr. Harry Kalos, Security Director for the Carmen Sisters. Now would you please join me in giving all these wonderful people a big, warm, Harlan welcome!

The applause was deafening, and lasted a full three minutes. Those on stage waved until their arms were tired. When the applause finally stopped, Mayor Knapp asked for comments from the governor, the economic secretary, Dr. Randy Peters, and lastly, from the Carmen Twins. All went well, but there was one strange occurrence during the governor's comments. Just after he started talking there was a muffled sound, and Sheriff Sterling's head seemed to bounce backward. Bert was a bit embarrassed when this happened, but he just smiled and got a puzzled look on his face. He then suddenly realized that the Pelle Anchor Cross he was wearing as a necklace felt very warm. He knew that something must have just taken place that could have resulted in harm or even death, but didn't because of the protective power of the anchor cross he was wearing. Just then the muffled sound could be heard again, and Bert's head again bounced back. And then the same sequence happened a third time. Bert's face turned red with embarrassment, but he felt no harm. Governor Shear paused in his remarks, turned to look at the sheriff and said, "You okay sheriff?" Bert nodded affirmatively and said, "Yes governor.....sorry", and the governor smiled and continued his remarks.

•••

"Damn, damn, damn," Badass shouted after firing three rifle shots directly at Sheriff Sterling's head. He slammed his rifle down on the floor of the van and started stomping on it in a fit of rage. Nothing was going as planned for him today. And he knew he didn't have a Plan C. He was so frustrated he decided to just leave his van and go home. It had been a terrible day. He reached for the door handle to open the back door to the van.

Deputy Simpson Brown had been on crowd control duty at the festival. Simpson had been standing close to Badass's van watching the afternoon ceremonies get underway. When Governor Shear began to speak he thought he heard a muffled sound and then noticed the sheriff's head jerk backward.

He looked around the crowd, but saw nothing out of the ordinary. Then he heard the same sound again, and again, and each time saw the sheriff's head jerk. After the third report he thought he caught something out of the corner of his eye moving on the side of the old van. He walked toward it, looking around.

Badass jerked open the van's back door and started to step out when he came face to face with Simpson Brown. Badass knew his day was getting ready to get even worse.

"Hey, Badass, what're you doing in that van?" asked Simpson.

"None of your damn business," Badass replied.

"Not so sure about that. I'd like to have a little look inside the van if you don't mind." Simpson said.

"You got no right to do that. I done nothing wrong," replied Badass

Simpson pulled out his revolver, pointed it at Badass, and said, "Then you got nothing to worry about. I just want to look around. I thought I heard a strange noise and saw something moving from the side of your van. Probably just my imagination, but just step back in there and let me have a quick look."

Badass complied. Simpson walked into the van and immediately saw the rifle on the floor. It looked like it had a silencer on it, and it's scope had been bent. Simpson said, "Well, well, what have we here? Looks like you've been doing a little shooting." He picked up the rifle, smelled it, and said, "Yep. Smells like it's just been fired. I think you need to spend the rest of the weekend in jail, and tell your story to Judge Oakes on Monday morning. I'm placing you under arrest for attempted murder."

"No way!" shouted Badass. "I just had that gun in my van for protection, and dropped it and it accidently discharged. I then got mad and stomped on it. I done nothing wrong."

"Try that story out on Judge Oakes on Monday," said Simpson. "But you better come up with why there's no hole in the van if the rifle discharged!"

"Had the back door open," Badass lied. "Bullet went flying out the door. Didn't leave no hole."

"Sounds bad to me, Badass, but Judge Oakes will decide."

Simpson then placed handcuffs on Badass, grabbed the rifle for evidence, closed the van's back door, and marched Badass off to the sheriff's department to be placed in a holding cell for the weekend.

●●●

After the speeches concluded, Mayor Knapp again took the podium and said, "Ladies and gentlemen, we've had a fine afternoon. We've heard from some very, very special people. I know you have enjoyed it as much as I have. But for the grand finale, I want to call five people back up, and ask that they stand in a row at the front of the stage. Each will be wearing one of the wonderful, beautiful, mysterious, and powerful golden anchor crosses. First, Deputy Kyle Potter found the very first anchor cross right here in Harlan County some 13 years ago. Kyle is wearing the Seibert Anchor Cross. Next I would like Sheriff J. Bert Sterling to join Kyle. Bert is wearing the anchor cross that was discovered by Dr. Randy Peters in Prato, Italy about two years ago. The Pelle Anchor Cross is owned by Domenico Pelle. The third anchor cross was discovered about a year ago by Pastor Raymond Bell while on a mission trip to the Seychelles archipelago in the Indian Ocean. The Helena Anchor Cross is owned by Felix Faure, and is worn today by Pastor Raymond Bell. Finally, the last two anchor crosses were discovered last spring by reporter Renee Dubois of the **Le Monde** newspaper in Paris. These two anchor crosses are owned by the Carmen Twins of Madrid, Spain, whom you have just met and had the honor to hear speak.

All five stood at the front of the stage proudly wearing an anchor cross. All the media present swarmed to get good pictures of the lineup. The crowd was orderly, but did press toward the stage to get a good look. The only noise to be heard was the clicking of camera shutters and the buzzing of video camera motors. After about 15 minutes Mayor Knapp again stood at the podium and announced that a couple more music groups would begin performing shortly. Those on stage began to leave.

Sheriff Sterling, Deputy Potter, Harry Kalos, and Trooper Ape Cornett gathered all five of the anchor crosses and took them back to the Seibert Anchor Cross Memorial where the public could continue to view them until the end of ACFes.

After Mayor Knapp had said his good-byes to the governor, the secretary, and Trooper Ape Cornett he left the stage and began to walk back to Creech Cafe. As he was walking through the crowd he ran into Fatso Chappel. Fred said, "Hey, Fatso, been a while since I saw you. Did ole Trigger give you the day off?"

Fatso replied, "Sure did. He said I needed to attend the festival. I sure have enjoyed it, Mayor Knapp."

"Well, thank you Fatso. Folks like you are what's made it a success. Tell Trigger I said hi."

"Will do," responded Fatso. "I'm headed now to get me one of those good chili dogs from the vendor over there. Hey Mayor, do you know the difference between an elephant and a loaf of bread?"

Mayor Knapp thought a moment, and then said, "No, Fatso, I guess I don't."

"Well, I guess I won't send you to the grocery," Fatso replied with a chuckle.

Fred continued walking to Creech Cafe, shaking his head.

Chapter 28

Harlan, Kentucky

Fred arrived back at Creech Cafe. He had invited all of the ACFes committee plus Randy's visitors to stop by Creech's for coffee and ice cream after their afternoon session at the festival. He had arranged for a large table to be set up in the back of his restaurant so the group could talk in relative privacy. Kyle and Carolyn Potter, Jake Keller, Raymond Bell, and Sheriff J. Bert Sterling were already seated when Fred walked in.

"Greetings my friends," Fred said as he pulled up a chair at the table. "If I'm counting correctly we're only missing Dr. Peters, the Carmen Sisters, Renee Dubois, and Harry Kalos. I feel sure they'll be along shortly. I'm sure that they were detained by the crowd wanting to talk and take pictures. I hope each of you enjoyed the day as much as I did."

Bert replied, "I can't speak for everyone, but I thought

it came off very nicely. Of course I got a big extra treat from the capture of the Junk Yard gang plus Eagle Eye Looney. Yes indeed, it was a super day for me."

"Hi friends, hi friends," Polly squawked as the five missing guests walked through the front door.

"Hi Polly," Randy replied, and reached up and gave Polly a nice pet.

"Thank you, thank you," Polly answered.

Randy, Harry, Renee, Elisabeth, and Henriette walked back to the table and greeted those already seated, and then took their seats.

Fred then proclaimed, "Well, hail, hail, the gang's all here! Thank each of you so much for honoring me by your presence in my humble establishment. I just thought that after such a great day at ACFes we could gather to talk and enjoy a little ice cream. And speaking of ice cream, I think it's just arrived."

Two of Fred's employees appeared carrying trays of ice cream sundaes. They delivered these and took drink orders.

Fred began, "Since we were all at the afternoon session, we know exactly what was said. The one thing that is a mystery to me was what caused the slight disturbance with the sheriff. So I'll just ask Bert if he could enlighten us a little."

Bert replied, "I'm glad to share what I know. But frankly, that's not a lot. The governor got up to speak and shortly after he began I heard a muffled sound that seemed to come from somewhere in the crowd, and then I felt what seemed like an impact of something hitting my head. Whatever it was, it caused my head to jerk back, and that's what people noticed. I wasn't hurt at all, and didn't feel any pain......my head just suddenly felt as though something hit it. I then became a bit more concerned because the Pelle Anchor Cross that I was wearing felt very warm, and I knew from past history that this always indicated that the wearer had been protected from bodily harm or even death. I guess I got a strange look on my face when I realized all this, and about that time I felt two more impacts to my head, and even more heat from the Pelle Anchor Cross. That's all I know about it. The governor took note, and asked if I was okay. That was it. Sure was strange."

Elisabeth then said, "Sheriff, I can tell you that my anchor cross also got very warm, and I'll bet the other three did as well." Elisabeth then looked at Henriette, Kyle, and Raymond. They all nodded in agreement. "So you are exactly correct. Someone, or some thing, was threatening us. Because you felt an impact, the danger was likely directed at you. But all of us on the stage were in jeopardy."

Kyle then spoke, "I think I can shed a little light on the incident. I had a call from Deputy Simpson Brown just as we were leaving the stage. He said that he had arrested Badass Brown. And incidentally, Simpson and Badass aren't related He said Badass was in the van parked there in front of Creechs, and that he had noticed something move from the side of the van at the same time of the muffled sounds and Bert's head movement. Simpson said he caught Badass coming out of the back of the van, and then found a rifle with a silencer lying on the floor of the van. The gun smelled like it had just been fired. Of course Badass denied it all, but Simpson placed him in a holding cell and he'll appear before Judge Oakes on Monday morning."

Randy said, "I think that clears it up. Badass was shooting at you, Bert, and those impacts were bullets bouncing from some kind of protective shield that was provided via the Pelle Anchor Cross. Fortunately, the deflected bullets must have traveled upward without hitting anyone or doing any other damage. Just be thankful you were wearing the anchor cross!"

"More than thankful," Bert replied. "The good Lord was certainly looking after me. Not many lawmen can say they survived three bullets coming right at their face!"

Fred then said, "That explains that! And all's well that ends well! Fortunately, the whole incident did not really even cause more than a slight pause in the program, Bert was protected by the Pelle Anchor Cross and was uninjured, and Badass was caught and is in jail. So much for which to be thankful!"

Renee Dubois then asked, "Do you think the explosion that took place over our car just as we were arriving for the afternoon session and the rifle shots could possibly be connected?"

Sheriff Sterling answered, "I've been thinking about that. I actually don't know. Just the fact that Badass Brown was in the area raises the possibility that they certainly could be. But we just don't have much to go on from the explosion. I've had one of my deputies searching the area and collecting all the debris he can locate for analysis. But I don't know if that will tell us anything or not. We'll just have to wait and see."

The mayor commented, "I have no idea either what that explosion was, but as it turned out the crowd thought it was some kind of fireworks as a part of the festival, and even applauded it. Again, as far as ACFes was concerned, the explosion was a plus. More thanks to those wonderful anchor crosses."

Fred pointed to an article recently printed in the **Harlan Daily Enterprise** that he had posted on the wall in the back of his restaurant and said, "I have to tell you the story behind that article."

Everyone glanced at the article and got grins on their faces. Bert said, "Okay Fred, let's hear it."

Fred began, "Those two guys pictured in the article live in Harlan. They had taken a trip to Knoxville, Tennessee and while walking down a street in downtown Knoxville noticed a sign in the window of a store that said 'Suits - $5 each, Trousers - $4.50 each, Shirts - $2.00 each'. One of the guys looked at the other and said, 'Those are great prices. Why don't we buy several of each and take them back to sell in Harlan.....we could make a lot of money!'. The other fellow approved, and they walked into the store. The clerk looked at them and asked if he could help them. The one fellow then said, 'Yes, we would like to purchase 10 suits, 10 trousers, and 10 shirts.' The clerk then said, 'I bet you boys are from Harlan.' The other fellow answered, 'As a matter of fact we are....how did you know that?' The clerk said, 'Because this is a dry cleaners!'"

Fred and his guests continued to enjoy their refreshments and conversation with each other. After about an hour the gathering dispersed. It had been a full and most interesting day.

Randy and his guests returned with Pastor Bell to his home for the evening, and the others went their separate ways. Tomorrow, Sunday, would be the last day of the festival. There would be a special service in the morning at New Hope Baptist Church in which Pastor Raymond Bell would address the special significance of the anchor crosses, and the Carmen Sisters would make remarks. Various musical groups would perform on the court house stage in the afternoon, and the Seibert Anchor Cross Memorial would be open from 1 to 6 pm.

Chapter 29

Harlan, Kentucky

New Hope Baptist Church was packed for the Sunday morning service. Prior to the service the Kentucky State Police security team assigned to guard the anchor crosses had brought them from the Seibert Memorial to the church. They would return them to the Memorial after the service so they could continue to be viewed by the public from 1 to 6 pm. Kyle Potter was wearing the Seibert anchor cross, Sheriff Sterling wore the Pelle, Pastor Bell the Helena, and the Carmen twins each had their anchor cross. Kyle, Bert, and the Carmen Twins sat with Harry Kalos, Renee Dubois, and the rest of the ACFes committee in the reserved front pew.

At exactly 11 am Pastor Raymond Bell stood from his chair behind the dais and walked to the pulpit to greet everyone to the morning service. After a prayer and the singing of two old hymns Raymond said, "Please allow me to say how very pleased I am to look out and see every seat filled in our church! I know we have many visitors this morning, and I appreciate each one of you, and sincerely hope that you will visit again soon. We have altered our normal Sunday morning worship service this morning to accommodate some very special guests. In just a minute I'll ask Elisabeth and Henriette Carmen to address you. But before I do, I would like to share some thoughts about the wonderful anchor crosses. I think each of you already are aware of the history of the Seibert, Pelle, and Helena anchor crosses, and now we have the final two that Constantine made and gave to Pope Sylvester I. Miraculously, all five of these truly remarkable artifacts have found their way to Harlan County, and are actually all here in this morning's service. I also feel certain that you know that Constantine made six of these anchor crosses, keeping one for himself and giving the other five to the Pope. I know that Dr. Peters will now be devoting a lot of his time at the Center for Appalachian Research to locating the final anchor cross, that belonging to Constantine the Great. But it is just mindboggling to me that the five he gave to Pope Sylvester I have been located, and are present with us today.

There's certainly a lot in this ole world that we don't understand. Thanks to the effort of Dr. Randy Peters, his research has shed much light on where these golden anchor crosses originated, and how they each have survived for almost 1700 years. Some 325 years before the artifacts were cast by Constantine in the shape of the anchor crosses, the gold from which they were made was in the form of bars which were blessed by our Lord Jesus Christ before He gave them to Saint Peter to help start the church.   One of these bars, called St. Peter's gold, was then given to Constantine by Pope Sylvester I around 325 AD to be used to make the six anchor crosses. These artifacts are not just simple inert jewelry. For reasons we don't now, and likely will never understand, they possess a power beyond this world. Each anchor cross has the inscription **Pax Tecum** on the cross's horizontal arm. **Pax Tecum** is Latin, and can be translated to mean 'Peace be with you'. Our Lord Jesus Christ was, is, and forever will be the Prince of Peace. Through means not understood by mortal man, the gold in these beautiful anchor crosses, having been blessed by our Lord, has the power to maintain peace for any person possessing one. This miraculous power has been demonstrated countless times, and Dr. Peter's research has documented many of these. The Harlan County pioneer Reverend Karl Seibert wrote in his diary that the golden anchor cross he wore prevented him from injury after falling over a high cliff in Virginia. That same Seibert anchor cross while being worn by Kyle Potter prevented the death of Kyle and his mother Carolyn, and several bank employees, during an attempted bank robbery here in downtown Harlan. On their return flight from Italy, Dr. Peters and Dominick Pelle along with everyone on the aircraft were saved from certain death by the intervention of the power in the anchor cross being worn by Randy Peters. And then when taken to Harlan the Pelle anchor cross was attributed to saving the life of a United States Senator when an assassin's attempt failed because of the presence of the mysterious anchor cross. The

Helena anchor cross was brought to Dr. Peters' center after having been discovered on a plantation in the Seychelles by Pastor Raymond Bell while on a mission trip. It's power was demonstrated on at least two occasions in which both a robbery and an attempt on the life of Sheriff Sterling were prevented.

And now, this morning the final two anchor crosses given by Constantine to Pope Sylvester I have been brought to our service by the twin sisters Elisabeth and Henriette Carmen. I know that they have stories to tell you about the mysterious and unexplainable power of their anchor crosses. Before I present them, I would just like to quote two verses of scripture. Hebrews 6:19 says, *'We have this hope* (meaning salvation through Christ) *as an anchor of the soul, sure and steadfast'*. And then First Corinthians 1:18 says, *'For the message of the cross is foolishness to those who are perishing, but to us who are being saved it is the power of God'*. I think in these two passages the Bible brings to light the significance of both the anchor and the cross, and those two are symbolized together in the beautiful Savior's Crosses. Truly, there is power in the Cross! And to think that we, in this small community of Harlan, Kentucky, have been witness to these beautiful artifacts that were blessed by our Lord Jesus Christ is simply astounding."

Pastor Bell then introduced the Carmen sisters, and they each talked briefly describing the history of their anchor crosses, their experiences with them, and how much they enjoyed working with Dr. Peters and their enjoyable trip to Harlan for the festival.

At the conclusion of the Carmen sisters' remarks, Raymond asked Kyle and Bert to come up and join him and the sisters. The five of them then stood across the front of the dais proudly wearing their anchor crosses. As they stood, Pastor Bell asked the congregation to stand and they all joined hands and sang one verse of Amazing Grace. The service concluded.

Chapter 30

Harlan, Kentucky

It was Monday morning. Judge Oakes entered the courtroom after the bailiff's announcement. He took his seat and asked for the first case.

"The people versus Brown," called the clerk.

Badass Brown approached and stood before the bench alone.

Judge Oakes then said, "Mr. Brown, you are charged with the attempted murder of Sheriff J. Bert Sterling. Do you not have an attorney?

"No judge....I'll represent myself."

"Very well, how do you plea," asked the judge.

"Not guilty, your honor. I was simply working in my van parked in front of Creech Cafe. I had a rifle for my protection. I accidently hit the rifle and it fell on the floor and discharged.

The back door to the van was open and the bullet sailed right out the back door. A few minutes later when I was leaving the van Deputy Simpson Brown stopped me and saw my rifle. He sniffed it and said it had been fired and placed me under arrest. I didn't do anything wrong Judge Oakes."

The judge replied, "Sounds fishy to me." He then looked over at the prosecuting attorney's table and said, "Mr. Smith, what say you?"

Daniel Smith, the prosecuting attorney, said, "Your honor, someone took three shots at Sheriff Sterling. Deputy Brown saw something move on the side of the van just as one of the shots was fired. He then caught Badass, pardon my language, trying to escape. He did smell the rifle and it had been recently shot. There's no doubt of Mr. Brown's guilt."

"So you say," said Judge Oakes. "But the fact is, it's his word against yours. You have no evidence to prove that he took shots at the sheriff."

Just as the judge was about to release Badass, the door through which those charged entered the court room swung open and in walked the town drunk, Bennie Sekao, followed by Deputy Kyle Potter. Bennie immediately saw Badass standing before the judge and shouted, "That's him. That's ole Badass. He's the one that made me help him try and drop that grenade on the sheriff's car. The whole thing was his fault. He made me put the drone in place, and when he got it all positioned right over the sheriff's car he tried to release the grenade. Something happened, and the damn thing exploded while it was still in the drone. Everything was Badass's fault. He made me help him."

Badass stood spellbound. His mouth dropped open, all the blood drained from his face, and his eyes got big as saucers. He then shouted at Bennie, "Shut your mouth, Bennie. You just made up that whole story."

Judge Oakes slammed down his gavel and shouted, "Order. I'll have order in this court.

Deputy Potter, would you kindly explain the meaning of this?"

Kyle then said, "Sorry for the intrusion, your honor, but we had arrested Bennie on charges of being drunk in public and assaulting Mrs. Harrison. Bennie had his water gun and squirted Mrs. Harrison in a very embarrassing spot. She called us on her cell phone and we responded and made the arrest. While he was drunk, he started spouting off about how Badass Brown had tried to drop a grenade from a drone on Sheriff Sterling. I thought I needed to have him here in court this morning so you could hear his story."

Judge Oakes said, "Thank you Deputy Potter. Please bring Mr. Sekao before the bench."

Kyle and Bennie walked before the Judge and stood next to Badass Brown. Badass looked at Bennie like he wanted to wring his neck.

The judge then said, "Good morning Mr. Sekao. Sounds like you've been hitting the bottle a little too heavy again."

"Just had a little snort, your honor," Bennie replied.

"And you squirted Mrs. Harrison," the judge said.

"I was just playing, judge. Didn't hurt a thing," Bennie responded.

Judge Oakes continued, "And then you told Deputy Potter that you helped Mr. Brown fly some sort of drone that was loaded with a grenade, and tried to drop it on Sheriff Sterling?"

"That's the honest truth, Judge Oakes. He made me do it. I didn't want to. I like Bert, but I didn't have no choice. Badass said he'd kill me if I didn't help him."

"That's a baldfaced lie, your honor," Badass shouted to the judge. "Bennie made up that story. He's the town drunk, and he likes to make up stories to hurt people. He's just mad because I wouldn't give him a bottle of booze. He's got nothing to prove what he just said."

"You got any evidence, Mr. Sekao?" asked the judge.

"Well, no, I guess not. That drone thing blew up," Bennie replied.

Judge Oakes said, "Okay. Mr. Brown, this is your lucky day. My guess is that you not only tried to shoot the sheriff with that rifle, but that you also tried to kill him by dropping a grenade from a drone. Bennie has told me some tales before that were hard to believe, but I don't think he made this one up. However, the fact is we have no evidence sufficient to hold you over for trial. So you are dismissed. Try and stay out of trouble."

"Thank you judge. Thank you. I'm going home and I swear I'll stay out of trouble," Badass said as he turned and left the courtroom.

The judge continued, "And as for you, Mr. Sekao, it would appear that you are now sober. Mrs. Harrison is not here to press assault charges against you, so I'll release you as well. You go home, stay away from the booze, and keep out of trouble."

"Yes sir, Judge Oakes. I sure will," Bennie said, and he too turned and left the court room.

"Next case," shouted Judge Oakes.

"The people versus Potter, Cawood, Anderson, Lingal, and Looney," announced the clerk.

The junk yard gang plus Eagle Eye Looney were marched before the bench.

Judge Oakes said, "Gentlemen, you are charged with using firearms to commit grand larceny. That's a very serious charge. Could get each of you at least 15 years in prison. Do you not have an attorney?"

Bad Eye Cawood spoke, "We ain't got no lawyer, your honor. But I guess we need one."

"You got that right," the judge said. "I will appoint a lawyer to represent you. You will appear again in my court one week from today to answer the charges. Bailiff, please return these five to jail."

The five were taken from the court room.

● ● ●

Monday afternoon found Mayor Knapp, Sheriff Sterling, and Deputy Potter having coffee at Creech Cafe.

Bert said, "Well Mr. Mayor, the first ACFes is now history. Everything considered, I think it was extremely successful.

I think the average person that came to attend went away feeling that his or her time and money were very well spent. And we had record numbers in town for all three days. The governor and secretary certainly thought it a big success, and I'd be willing to bet that state funding for next year's festival will likely be increased."

"Thanks, Bert," the mayor replied. "I believe what you say is correct. Overall, it exceeded my expectations. The numbers were certainly there. But to me the most important thing was the exceptional participation by the Carmen Sisters, by Randy, and by all the ACFes committee members. That really was what made it such a giant success. Harlan, and Harlan County, were well represented. I think those attending this year will go back home and tell their friends and relatives what a grand time they had, and this will result in an even larger ACFesII."

Kyle then said, "Mr. Mayor, how in the world are you going to handle more people. I thought the town was about to capacity this year!"

"Oh, I think we can always squeeze in a few more," Fred said with a smile.

Bert said, "I think a big draw for this year was having the Carmen Twins participate with their anchor crosses. What would be the big draw for next year?"

Fred replied, "I don't know right now. We've got a little time to put that together, but I have a suspicion that Randy is probably back at his center this afternoon trying to put together some kind of plan for locating that 6th anchor cross. Who knows, he just might be successful in finding it in time for next year's festival. That would sure be some draw..... Constantine's own anchor cross!! We'd probably have folks lined up from here to Pineville if that came to pass."

"I don't think I'd make plans on that," Bert said. "It could happen, but the Constantine anchor cross has not shown up since his death in 337 AD. The likelihood of it surfacing before next October is not real good."

"One can dream," Fred replied. "Speaking of Randy, I talked to him around noon today and he told me that all his guests got off this morning. He certainly sounded very pleased with the results of their visit."

"All those folks were just super," Kyle replied. "I certainly enjoyed meeting and talking with Harry Kalos. He's a first class security guy. I think the Carmen Sisters are in very good hands."

"I agree," Bert said. "And I sure want to get the copies of **La Monde** that have Renee's stories. Every time I looked at her during their visit here she was scribbling something in her note pad and had her recorder going. I think she also got some great pictures. I would predict the circulation for **La Monde** will likely skyrocket due to her articles."

"I wouldn't disagree," replied Fred.

Bert then said, "Having said all that good stuff about the festival, it did have it's moments. Badass Brown certainly could have caused major problems. And that Junk Yard Gang together with Eagle Eye Looney could have given ACFesl a black eye if they had been successful in robbing DiamondCraft during the parade."

"Yes indeed. Those could have been major problems. But they were not," Fred replied. "The good Lord was watching out for us. Many people could have been killed or badly injured. We were indeed very fortunate."

Kyle asked, "So what do you think will happen to the Junk Yard Gang and Eagle Eye Looney?"

Bert said, "I think come next Monday that Judge Oakes will throw the book at all of them. There will likely be a trial, but with all the eyewitnesses I just don't think they have a chance to get off. Bad Eye and his three buddies will likely get at least 15 years in the slammer. For Eagle Eye, things could be even worse. Not only was he caught red handed at DiamondCraft, but they also want him in Lexington for robbing that jewelry store there. I wouldn't be surprised to see old Eagle Eye out of circulation for 20 years at least."

"Justice will be rendered," Fred replied.

"For them, yes," said Kyle, "but ole Bennie and Badass got off scott free."

"That is somewhat troublesome," Bert responded. "For Bennie, I don't feel so bad. But I just feel certain that ole Badass was trying every way possible to do me in. If it hadn't been for Bennie blabbing everything to Kyle and then to Judge Oakes, we likely would never have known that Badass had tried to drop a grenade from a drone. And I don't think there's any doubt that he then tried to shoot me with that rifle. I just thank the good Lord that I was protected by wearing the Pelle anchor cross. Unfortunately, there just wasn't any real evidence against him. But we'll be keeping an eye on ole Badass."

Fred grinned and said, "Yeah, and all you have to do to put the fear of God into ole Bennie is to just tell him you're going to sick Preacher Puss on him!

The three good friends laughed and slapped each other's backs.